DATE EXPECTATIONS

A MATCHMAKER NOVELLA

HOPE BOLINGER

TREY SOTO

Beatrice & Co. Books

DATE EXPECTATIONS BY HOPE BOLINGER and TREY SOTO

Published by Beatrice & Co. Books

Cover Design by Hope Bolinger and Angela Lynum

PaperbackISBN: 978-1-968575-02-1

Ebook ISBN: 978-1-968575-01-4

DEDICATION (TREY SOTO)

This book is dedicated to my ex-girlfriends. Your words and actions hurt me beyond what you can imagine, and for that, I say thank you. Through therapy and grief recovery, you made me realize how important it was to stand up for myself, to acknowledge what was and was not my fault, and to know what was best for me.

DEDICATION (HOPE BOLINGER)

This book is dedicated to all the wonderful Christian men I have interacted with over the years. Dating is the absolute worst for everyone, and I am deeply sorry for what you have gone through as well.

I

NEON PAPERS

NOAH

Noah Brandon was certain the neon posters would burn his eyes out. But the theater department had run out of the white printer paper, so he'd have to make do.

He tacked one of the Do-Good posters onto the corkboard and planted his hands on his hips as he stepped back to make sure it hadn't gone crooked under the red pin.

During the cast's first rehearsal for *Matchmaker*, their director had fluttered the posters in every which way, like a senior chucking up his homework papers on the last day of school. Noah would know. He'd graduated high school four years ago, and the hallways had been a mess on the last day of senior year.

"Post these anywhere you can. I love that we're having people do acts of kindness for our fall play promotion." Every year, the school would drum up reasons for the students to see the scholarship play—the play that would allow one student pursuing theater at Mansfield Christian College to attend the school for free.

Although Noah wasn't sure what doing good actions had

to do with Thornton Wilder's play about a matchmaker, he decided not to question it. Anything to get butts in seats, and well, *it wouldn't hurt the school to be a little kinder to each other.*

So he'd gotten right on it. A week after his internship had ended with the local theater, he'd jumped straight into his senior year with the school theater. Hoped all the "dues" he paid of late nights and volunteer opportunities at various theaters would end up in a job somewhere in the local thespian circuit.

A screeching noise emanated from the coffee shop in the Student Center (TSC). Cinnamon chai greeted his nostrils moments later.

As he moseyed to the column that supported the second floor above them to tack on a poster with some tape, he spotted a figure in his periphery. He'd recognize that straight, black hair anywhere.

Emerson "Em" Levi waved at him.

"Long time no see."

He grinned and scooped her up into a hug as she approached. Somehow, she smelled of cinnamon, just like the chai.

He...liked that scent.

Nope, stop it. He wagged a finger in his noggin as he released her from the embrace. *You're not going to be dating anyone your senior year, let alone your best friend.* He dragged his fingers through his curls, hoping she hadn't caught onto the emotional slip in his expression. She hadn't appeared to.

Em vanished for a moment to retrieve her drink from the coffee shop. She returned and squeaked her straw up and down in the lid. "Good summer?"

"Eh."

He recounted the internship he had to pay for—*thanks for that, Practicum credits*—at a local theater. Corralling kids for their drama camp and handling more meltdowns than an ice cream salesman on a hot summer day.

"I was hoping that it could lead to something...maybe a job with them that I could slide into right after second semester, but—"

But they'd already stuffed the theater board full of people who didn't look like they'd retire anytime soon. Had positions from technical director to scenic designer covered. Although they promised him a position for their drama camp next year —this time with a stipend—the money wouldn't even cover rent for a month in a studio apartment.

No, not even in cornfield-laden Indiana.

Em sipped. "Huh, so how did that go?"

He explained that he didn't want to be in the presence of children for some time, which sent her chuckling.

"Yeah, sounds about right. Too bad every guy and girl here on campus wants a big family, right?" Em rolled her eyes.

Air hissed between Noah's teeth. Not *every* guy and girl. Not that he would know...he didn't plan to date until he landed on his feet after graduation. Stirred up way too much drama in the theater department to try to pursue a relationship with one of the thespians. After all, they all tended to get cast in the same parts. If two main characters had beef with each other, the audience members would be able to tell.

And if I tried to date a non-theater person, they'd get on me for how much time I spend in rehearsals. He'd witnessed it one too many times with some of his other actors. Seen one too many a breakup in the green room or backstage area over cast members not having enough time for their significant others.

He switched the subject to the Do-Good fundraiser, and their conversation dwindled to a natural close. Em saluted him and headed back to her table to stalk a couple she'd lately matched. He tried not to seethe as he went back to hanging up posters. To think a girl with talents like hers had tried to make money off of desperate couples through her matchmaking business.

You can do so much more with the kind of talents you have, Em.

Something buzzed in his pocket, and he dug out his phone. Eyebrows threaded together as he spotted the caller ID.

What's the director from the summer camp doing calling me?

Hope fluttered in his chest. Maybe a spot would open up, and he could get a job before the first semester even started. He swiped the green button. "Hello?"

"Hey!" Sarah Yaeger sounded out of breath. Considering she often forced her tangled hair into a ponytail that strained against the frizz, everything in her demeanor read rushed. He'd assumed it was because she, too, had to manage dozens of children for the summer alongside him. She'd directed the theater camp this last summer and directed several shows at that same theater.

She sounds flustered. But maybe that's just how she always is.

"Got some time to talk, Noah?"

"Yeah." He perched at a table as a student bustled by with a noisy salad container that he shook. "Just hanging up some stuff for our theater. I can wait to do that until later."

"Okay, so I need to start this thing by saying we don't have a position for you."

He deflated and forced his attention on a student who strummed his guitar nearby. Three girls flanked the guitar player's sides. Noah should've known better than to get his hopes up. A theater job in a podunk place like this? Slim chance.

"Okay..." He coughed the disappointment out of his tone. Poor Sarah. He'd probably asked her about seven different times this summer if there were any openings she knew of within a thirty-mile radius.

Leave it to me to try to find theater work in Indiana.

Even with his father's successful dentistry practice, he didn't see much of that money from his family's bank account. His parents had set some aside for schooling but made it *clear* they didn't approve of the career field he endeavored to pursue. And considering most theater opportunities rested in New York or out-of-price-range cities, he'd hoped for something closer to the school.

Hoped being the operative word.

"But." The lilt in Sarah's voice shot up. "I do have an opportunity for you, come next summer."

He leaned forward until his stomach hurt from doubling over. "Cool, I'm listening."

"So you know how we've been trying to get the local young playwright series going? Since there are tons of creative writing students at your school alone who like to do scripts?"

As his forehead wrinkled, he tried to remember the conversation they'd had sometime in June about this. Ah, yes, the same day a kid whacked him with a pool noodle during an acting exercise. Sarah had odd timing when it came to business ideas.

"Sure. But." He paled. "I'm not exactly a writer."

"That's okay. I know there are tons of students who can edit your stuff—pretty sure I've paid a few for some of my master's papers. But we have a grant to be able to do this. And the board would like someone who is on the inside to write that script for us. At least the first time we do it. Maybe we'll open it up to students if it runs well."

His mind swam. It wasn't unusual for theaters to work with insiders only for riskier ideas, but...

Does she want me to create a play for her?

What would he write about? He'd toyed with the idea of translating *The Simiarilion* to the stage or some fantasy book about dragons and elves—but knowing the theater banked off of productions like *Sound of Music* and *Fiddler on the Roof,* that wouldn't swing.

"Oh." Wow, brilliant. Call him Shakespeare with his eloquent responses.

"We'd pay you for it, with the grant, of course. Maybe a month's worth of work."

Dryness filled his throat, and his tongue stuck to the roof of his mouth. A month's worth? Maybe that would be enough to put a downpayment on an apartment's rent and impress his parents enough to lend him a few hundred bucks to buy him some time. He could slide his way into the theater if he succeeded enough with this.

If being the other operative word.

"Erm. What do you guys want the play to be about? Any themes?"

For the first time in the three months he'd known her, Sarah paused.

But only for a second. "Well, we're kicking off a production of *Working*—you know, the play all about people doing ordinary jobs—and it got me thinking—what if we have a story set now, in the modern-day—"

Got it. J.R.R. Tolkien is out. Too bad most of his ideas had to do with fantasy worlds.

"—involving something to do with the college or young adult experience. Especially since the grant is for a young playwright, it makes sense, right?"

Sure.

If he hadn't spent every waking moment in the theater, he might have a pulse on what ailed college students. Yeah, he knew the dorms fell apart every two seconds—living in one of the worst buildings on campus himself. But because he'd spent so much time in the auditorium...

Maybe I should ask around. Get some ideas.

He credited Sarah for the idea to have one of the professional writing students edit his play. He'd pay them, of course. Maybe with a few hands on deck, he could pull this thing off.

Sarah's voice pulled him back. "Anyway, I've gotta go. We have a board meeting coming up in fifteen minutes, and I haven't had any food in me all day. Keep me posted, and at the latest, we need that play by April. You can send it to me in snippets in the meantime."

A rattled breath trailed his lips when she hung up. April. That sounded far away enough not to send his knees knocking. But if he knew anything about how school years flew by, it would be less time than he imagined. He scooped up the papers in his hands and moved to the next column, burning his brain for ideas.

"Hey, need help with that, man?"

With a piece of tape caught between his teeth, Noah glanced up and saw a bulky guy with a swath of brown hair on his head.

"Dylan?" He pressed the tape onto the top of the paper. The wetness of his mouth must've ruined it because the poster fluttered down. "How have things been?'

They clapped into a bro hug, and his friend Dylan recounted his summer.

Before this past summer, Noah had met him backstage for several shows, where Dylan volunteered with the deck/stage crew. But Dylan had withered away from the theater last year when his psych assignments took over his schedule.

Dylan paused and glowered at a girl who passed by. When she caught his gaze, her face turned scarlet, and she huddled into the group of friends around her.

"Are you—?" *Is it worth asking?* Dylan could talk anyone's ear off. "—okay, man?"

Dylan sighed, shoved his hands into his pockets, and shook his head. "Allison."

Noah frowned and tilted his head. Didn't ring any bells. There were a lot of girls at this university who had names that went somewhere along the lines of Allison.

Another sigh from Dylan. "She messed me up last year." He was strangely not talkative today.

Ah. Noah did recall something about Dylan blushing over a girl backstage. He'd often brought his phone back there to swipe through a dating app, much to their director's chagrin.

Awkwardness hung in the air between them.

"Wanna talk about it?" Noah wasn't sure if he regretted asking this question, but it felt rude not to throw it out there.

At first, Dylan jerked his head, then paused.

"Actually, yeah, it might be good to get off my chest. Are you sure you're okay with hearing this?"

Noah parked in a seat and gestured at Dylan to begin. Who knew? Maybe this could help inspire that play.

2
SHORT KINGS
DYLAN

To be honest, college has been an eye-opener in the dating realm. I never thought it would be this tricky, let alone shallow.

I went on a few dates with people, but there was always this weird game you had to play. The moment you walk into it, they immediately size you up. How you look, how you talk, how you laugh...you get the picture. I even had to be careful of showing my "true self" in my interests and hobbies, or that would be a turn-off. People used to tell me to hold off on letting out, well, me, until the third or fourth date.

Who would've guessed I would be judged for what I enjoyed?

A group of students started a dating app for the surrounding colleges. I met someone named Allison. As it turned out, we had a few classes together. She was a sweet person and incredibly smart. We both took Psych 101 in our freshman year and had a few group projects together. We weren't exactly friends, but we knew each other. I decided to connect with her on the app, wondering why my thumb shook so much when I swiped on her, and to my surprise, she responded.

> Allison: You were in my group project, right?
> How have things been :)

WE TALKED A LOT THE FOLLOWING DAYS AND HAD MORE IN common than I expected.

After talking for a week, I thought we should catch up over coffee. Despite our class schedules being polar opposites, we found a spot on a Friday morning and met up at Common Grounds, the preferred coffee shop for Mansfield students.

Knowing how dating is over here, I chose to pay for the coffee and initiated the conversation, especially when it came to her interests. "You're going into psych. Tell me more about that."

For some reason, she liked that. "No guy ever wants a career woman. And then boom." She made an explosion with her hands. "There you are."

Overall, we had a good time, and we hit it off well to where a second date was already in mind. I couldn't believe it.

Did I just score a second date...with her? I hadn't had luck with dating. I felt like I was under a microscope whenever I came face-to-face with a female. But with her? Not so much.

I didn't even have to wait for that fourth date to show her me...the real me.

In the following weeks, we had a good time getting to know each other more and even went on a double date with my roommate and his fiancée.

"My dude." My roommate slapped me on the back after

and winked. "Y'all had more chemistry than even we did on our first date."

As time passed, though, I felt a shift in her overall presence. She seemed aloof as if she wanted to be anywhere but with me. At first, I assumed it was school, given that midterms were coming up. It wasn't just in our dates but in our texts and calls. I was doing more of the initiating and at one point....

Allison: My gosh...you text a lot.

Allison: Mind scaling it back a bit? LOL

IT JUST FELT WEIRD. I WAS DOING EVERYTHING RIGHT—AT least, according to the guys on my floor. I was going at her pace, giving her space, and trying not to pry too much. As it lingered on, however, I felt that maybe I should say something.

If there is one thing I have learned in the dating world, it is that standing up for yourself as a guy isn't welcome. If you're a woman? By all means, stand up for yourself and know your worth.

If you're a guy? It's seen as controlling, hostile, or aggressive. Sometimes even threatening. Granted, there are men like that out there, but they are exceptions and do not represent the rest of us.

So, I chose to say something. I figured I could at least have a sit with her and ask more in-depth about what she was getting at.

Dylan: Coffee? Friday? Tried to keep it to one text :)

Allison: Sure.

Huh weird. She always does periods when she's mad at someone.

Given how midterms were pressing more, I figured she would at least look forward to a break. As any man can guess, when you get a period at the end of a one-word text, you know you either messed up or that they have something up their sleeve.

An hour before we met, my anxiety shot through my ribcage. I couldn't sleep at all—my heart would race, and whatever sleep I managed to scrounge played nightmare scenario after scenario. Even with melatonin, I only managed three hours of sleep. As I padded over, I saw her sitting already at a high-top table.

Okay, let's see if I can figure out what I did wrong. Maybe pushed her too much?

I backtracked everything I could think of that would have made her mad. Maybe it was my assertiveness of wanting to talk after all. *I knew you should've held off on the more "you" bits until the third or fourth date.*

When I reached her table, her eye contact was a glance only for her to look down. *But what's there to feel guilt over?* I wasn't mad at her, nor was I looking to end it. *I'm just trying to understand what's happening.* I went in to get tea to help calm me down. My heart raced to where I could hear the uneven pattern surging through my ears. Jitters filled my hands as I grabbed my jasmine tea.

This is it, the moment I had been dreading for days. *Can't avoid it now.*

I sat, trying to analyze what I could about her. We had a moment of awkward silence that felt like an eternity. Amid the morning rush, the only sound I could hear was ringing in my ears. I spaced out, staring at my tea, which rippled due to the sound of the crowded line and blasting music. I didn't notice she had called for me until she said my name louder.

"Dylan! Seriously? First, you text too much, and now I can't get a word out of you?"

I snapped to reality.

We had some small talk, which felt nothing short of forced. I thought five times about just heading out and forgetting the whole thing. My gut clenched whenever I mused about that. *No, that's the coward's way.*

Then, I embraced the inevitable.

"I just want to know what's going on. I feel that you've gotten distant, and it seems that despite what I've tried, it feels like you keep pushing me away."

Her body language said it all. Shrugged shoulders, hardly touching her food, hands to herself, lack of eye contact, the shebang.

Ah. I caught on. "Hey, are you okay? Talk to me, Allison."

She went silent again. Tension filled the space between us as we heard laughter from the students in line to place their orders.

She leaned forward with her hands clasped together.

Oh gosh. Here goes... I wasn't sure what to anticipate or what she would say.

"Dylan, you are a very sweet guy. You have a good heart and have been active in looking out for me." Another silence stood between us as she opened her mouth, closed it, and opened it again. "But I just don't see it working out."

At first, I was nervous that I pressed too hard. At that moment, however, I blinked several times, fighting the temptation to claw earwax out of my ears.

She wants to break us up for no reason?

"So...did I do anything wrong?"

She shook her head. "No, trust me, you've been amazing. You've looked out for me...been so sweet. You're, like, an absolute dream."

Not amazing enough to keep around.

I brushed the thought away with a head-jerk. "Anything else you're not telling me?"

Another head shake.

I kept my voice low from the line behind us. "Nothing you're saying is making sense. You say I'm not doing anything wrong; you say that I treated you well and looked out for you. What's the problem, then?"

She didn't hesitate. "Because you're short."

I stopped to take in her words. "Umm, what?"

Blush formed on her cheeks, and she hunched into herself. "I know that sounds petty, but—"

"Hold on, what do you mean by that?" Insecurity crept into my shoulders, and I felt them hunch too. *Does every girl see me this way? Was she the only one gutsy enough to say something?*

She sighed. "I thought it wouldn't bother me at first, but now it does. You're not tall enough."

No one had said this to me...not in the dating field, that is. Sure, got the occasional short king joke, but never like this. "So let me get this straight. I'm 'perfect,' except I'm not tall enough?" *Should I wear heels to make her feel better?*

"Dylan, I want a man who will be able to protect me physically. You're, what, 5 foot 7? How is that gonna compare with other couples? Or how about if a taller guy was threatening me?"

I responded that we are in one of the safest cities in the county, and anything like that happening was one in a hundred. Not to mention, plenty of wrestlers and short kings can hold their own in matches. It's about agility and speed, not height. She shook her head.

"It's what I want. I don't feel safe with someone who can't protect me physically."

"So you're breaking up with me about something I have zero control over?"

Once again, her mouth opened and closed like a fish gasping for air. She settled on the following: "People are allowed to have preferences. Guys want women who just stay at home all the time and are super skinny. And you don't see me complaining when I refuse to date those people."

How fair is it that I am automatically disqualified for how I was born? I smeared a hand on my face and looked at her. She was no longer attractive to me. What did I ever see in her?

"I appreciate you showing your true colors, Allison. It goes a long way."

"Dylan! That's not—"

I got up and left.

Guess it takes some people longer than four dates to show the real them.

3
TRAUMA ICE CREAM
NOAH

"I think I've been traumatized."

Noah's veins froze in his dorm room after he picked up the call from Em. He bolted upright in bed as his roommate cast an eyebrow-narrowed glance his way. That lasted no more than two seconds as the roommate whipped his head back to continue playing GTA. Images flickered on their large TV, which sat on their two dorm-assigned desks.

Noah turned back to the receiver. "What happened?"

She laughed and said something about a bad date. Yeesh, he'd heard a lot about those lately. Ever since his run-in with Dylan at the Student Center, he'd caught snippets of other stories from guys in his dorms, guys at the theater...

All of them clutched in the claws of a cruel summer romance or recovering from the dregs of a bad breakup from last semester.

Maybe I should *write the play about that.*

He penciled the idea in his brain to do later...*after this call.* Maybe he could write a few samples and get the script Sarah's way. And maybe she could talk him out of it from that alone, so he didn't invest too much time into this. He probably wasn't that good of a writer, anyhow.

Em's voice brought him back. "Can you go to that ice cream shop?" The one near campus? Via car, he could arrive there in five minutes. He'd have to give up his coveted parking spot since the campus deemed it unnecessary to have enough spaces on campus versus the number of vehicles students owned—*gotta eke more money out of us from the parking tickets we get...*

But for Em, he'd park two miles away from his dorm, even in the heat of summer or frostbite of winter.

"Be there in five."

He made it in four and placed an order of mozzarella sticks in the compact shop. The line had trailed out the door, so they wouldn't call his food order in for...

"Order for Noah."

Huh, that was fast. It often took them half an hour for any fried foods. Maybe they'd made it for someone else, and that person never picked it up.

Or had made a batch for themselves and decided to give it away to the next customer who ordered it.

Grease stained his fingertips as he met Em, who huddled at the back of a booth. Poor thing. Even in the dim lighting, unnatural shadows were cast on her face. Maybe she'd seen a ghost.

"Tell me everything."

She bit her lip. "Okay, so I may have done something stupid."

He frowned. That start to a conversation never went well. Noah swirled his mozzarella stick in marinara sauce and brought it to his lips. Breading crumbled down his chin, and his stomach buckled. He'd regret these food choices five years from now, but who cared?

"Go on."

"So I have a new apartment-mate. I think I told you about her. Not the weird, adork-able one, or my girl bestie, but the other one who wears sports bras and yoga pants all the time."

"Jana, yeah. The one who can't stand you and flaunts her boyfriend all the time."

Em smirked and shoveled a buckeye candy from her ice cream mound into her mouth. "The one and only, but she called me a fraud and said if I couldn't prove that I—" She gestured at herself, smearing vanilla ice cream in her hair. "—could find a spouse, being the matchmaker I am, that I should refund every person I've ever helped in the past. To make matters worse, Jana said that she needed to be the one to set up dates for me."

He pinched his nose. *Em, please tell me you asked her to call off the bet.*

Yes, he had issues with her matchmaking business. But Jana? Seriously? Finding a perfect match at their campus was like convincing a professor who "didn't believe in giving out As on report cards" to give their students a 100 on the final exam.

Never going to happen.

Flush crawled up her neck. "I'm not proud of it. Anyway, she set up a date for me tonight, and he was." She rubbed her thumbs over her closed eyes as if attempting to wipe the memories away. "Awful."

Noah fought the urge to grab her hands, to still them, rub them.

Comfort them.

Dude, seriously, stop.

"Wanna talk about it?"

She snickered. "Sure. What do we want to discuss? The fact that he told me a woman's only calling it to pop out babies, or the fact that he nearly slammed me against the brick wall and yelled at me when I paid for myself."

Anger surged, boiling hot, up his spine. "He did WHAT?"

"Calm down." She waved her hands up and down, and despite her smile, her facial features pulled tautly. Eyes lasered him from every direction. Sometimes, he forgot how much theater gave him the ability to project.

He uttered a sorry and gestured for her to continue.

"Anyway, if this date taught me anything, it's two things. One." She tallied a finger. "Men are trash." She tossed him an apologetic glance. "Most are, not all."

He fought the urge to duke it out on that point.

If anything, from what he heard from the guys in his dorm, women topped some pretty Worst-Person-Ever lists too.

"And two, it solidifies why I do what I do. Quality control. I screen the couples ahead of time to make sure we don't have any wild cards in the mix. No, I'm not perfect, but I'm sure I can do better than most dating apps."

Eh, he wouldn't argue against that. Memories surged from his encounter with Dylan—he'd met on one of those apps... and *look where that got him.*

At least Em has her heart in the right place, even if her execution had gone askew.

"So why did you agree to this bet?"

She sighed and mentioned how Jana had a decent following and could put her business under. Even if Em didn't agree to the bet, maybe her past customers would demand their money back.

"I mean, it would look super cowardly of me to back down from something like this. If I'm not willing to go on dates, then why should I be setting people up on dates in the first place, you know?"

He shook his head and crunched into a now-cold mozzarella stick. Not only would Em have to date these awful guys Jana set her up with, but by the end of the school year, she'd have to marry one of them.

I wonder if there's another way we can tackle her student debt. The whole reason she'd started the matchmaking business in the first place. *Maybe a GoFundMe.*

He jotted down that idea next to the one about the play as they continued the conversation. Em frowned at her now buckeye-less ice cream and passed him a side, half-moon smirk.

"Anyway, I appreciate you grounding me." She gripped his hand and squeezed. "You always have a way of doing that. Making me feel safe."

More than once, when she'd helped out with a theater rehearsal, he had escorted her back to the dorm. Due to some Title IX issues that had plagued the campus the year before they enrolled, he didn't want to take any chances.

She stood, brushed some ice cream smears off her blue dress, and he watched the tremble in her fingertips.

"Want me to walk you back to the dorms, Em?"

She considered this for a moment. "Nah, I'll probably phone Harmony—" Her other apartment-mate, the weird one. "Or Laila." Apartment-mate number four and the girl bestie. "Whoever picks up, to keep me company. I've been talking your ear off enough as it is."

"You sure?"

She waved him off. "It's still early enough that people will see me walk back. It's not fully dark yet."

True. Had the sky darkened into an inky black, he would've insisted. But his shoulders weighed heavy with her words. *I need a few more minutes to process this.*

They said their goodbyes, and Em ducked out of the ringing door.

A figure took her place: lumpy, dark-circled eyes and a slumped posture in a jean jacket. Noah frowned. He knew the floormate, Lincoln, in a vague sense. The way someone remembers a candle scent from one they smelled in a store years ago.

But he did know, in more than a vague sense, that Lincoln intended to propose to his girlfriend tonight. The entire floor whooped and hollered, in togas, on his way out two hours ago.

Guess it didn't go well, based on how he's looking.

Noah half made up his mind to leave the poor soul alone when they locked eyes. Lincoln started toward him.

Shoot. No going back now as the man trudged toward the table. He slid himself inside, and Noah gestured at the front counter—where a worker jostled a silver milkshake cup in a machine.

"Want me to grab you something?"

Lincoln threw up a large hand. "No, it's fine." Then he drummed his fingertips on the table. "She said no, by the way."

Noah whistled. "I'm sorry. That sucks."

And he meant it. He watched his older brother go through a broken-off engagement. Heck, he'd brought that up to Em just a few minutes ago, begging her to somehow back out of the bet. But she apparently couldn't.

"Yeah." Lincoln rubbed either the soreness or the sprouting of tears out of his waterline. "I don't even know why I'm putting this on you—it's so humiliating to think about, but—"

Noah nodded.

He'd gotten this more than once, that he had a face that seemed to understand, that seemed to listen. His RA had begged him to be the discipleship leader on their floor: to lead guys in prayer and Bible studies. Had his theater schedule not interfered with what most people called "life," he would've taken him up on it.

Noah was always a good listener. Gave off the best non-judgy vibes. In another life, he would've made a good therapist.

Bet my parents would've been happy with that decision. Makes a whole lot more money than theater.

"I'm here to listen if you need." Noah rolled his shoulders back as if to knock off the weight Em had just put on him and make room for one more.

❧ 4 ❧
UPFRONT AND DISHONEST
LINCOLN

As you can imagine, churches can get pushy for newlyweds to have kids right away. I honestly met a couple who were already expecting in their first six months of marriage, and it just baffled me. I never judged couples like that, but that never seemed to go both ways.

"We just couldn't wait to start a family. Yes, this is an expensive state, but God always provides."

They were moving to California at the time, to the heart of San Francisco. Lord knows how they were going to pay the rent. *You hardly have the experience of learning to live together.* Not that I wanted to test God. I knew He helped people through all kinds of binds. But I'm sure He didn't tell every single couple to have kids the minute the honeymoon ended.

I held my thoughts to myself. I'd seen one of them, or both at the same time, turn a special color of red whenever anyone asked them why they didn't give their marriage one year before going for kids.

My parents and I would fight on and off about having kids.

"Don't you want to have kids? Who is going to take care

of you when you're old? Kids are a blessing, and I just don't understand how your generation got this warped idea that they're anything but that. I was scared when I had you, but that didn't stop me." Mom had folded her arms so tightly across her chest that I thought she'd saw her midsection in half.

Of course I wanted children. I just wanted to wait a few years into marriage so I could enjoy growing with an eventual wife. I'd watched my parents nearly get a divorce over the fact they didn't know each other well when they got married. With a ten-year age gap between them, Mom hardly understood who she was when she got married at eighteen. Young couples made it work; I'd seen it. But I knew it would take much more work, especially with a child in tow.

"Whatever plan you have, God's plan always succeeds yours." Mom had lifted her nose in the air when she'd said this, as if she'd imparted the most sage advice in the world. *How does she know what God's plan is for me?*

She wasn't wrong, biblically speaking, but given that she had me and my siblings right away, it doesn't surprise me that she thinks that way about families. It turns out that many families and women think this way in Midwest America, regardless of whether they're married or not.

When it came to dating, it was rather hard. What I wanted was a deal-breaker among most women. Except for a few who wanted "independence," but they wanted independence in all respects. They'd hardly respond to texts and would get bored with me fast. To top it off, a lot of women I dated craved to be stay-at-home moms. No ifs, ands, or buts about it.

Some were appalled at the very idea of a man making them work at all, even before bringing kids into the picture.

And while I respected SAHMs, the career path I'd chosen would make a living on one salary difficult for a family.

How do they expect me to provide for a whole family on a Worship Pastor salary?

That's why Jessica gave me a sense of hope. We first met through a dorm room date event on my floor. We had common interests—like playing Super Smash Bros. She would call me Link for short. That was her favorite character. And worship music—and we enjoyed our time together. After a few dates, I decided to ask the question, the one that would scatter so many away. But better now than to find out five years into a marriage.

"Hey, so I like you, but there's something absolutely essential for me."

She leaned forward and rested her chin on her hands. "Go on."

"Listen, I do want a family. I think kids are important. But it's also important for a married couple to grow in their few years together." I blushed. "I saw my parents go through a lot since they had my siblings and me right away. I want a family...but I want to get on my feet first. Have both people work some jobs so we could save up and build a beautiful life for them."

I, of course, told her that was well over a year down the road and just wanted to throw that out there. Not that I'd pictured wedding bells at that point.

She didn't even hesitate. "I appreciate you telling me early on. That's not an easy thing to get off your chest."

I was surprised at how well she took it, let alone responded. I blinked and made sure I'd heard it right. *She... she's not upset?*

At first, I felt skeptical, but she reaffirmed what she said later that night after I dropped her off back at her dorm. "Seriously, thank you for telling me the truth. I don't think what you're asking for is too much."

I shot her a text, and she answered right away, unlike those "independent" girls who'd play phone tag.

Lincoln: I had a great time tonight. It honestly means so much that you appreciate how I feel about this.

Jessica: And I appreciate that you trusted me and were honest :)

Lincoln: Aww. And you're sure you're okay with this?

Jessica: Of course, Lincoln. Yes, I want kids, but I'm not expecting you to be like me in every way. If that's what you need…a couple of years before we start a family…then I can adjust to that!

From then on, we had a steady year-and-a-half of dating. Whenever we talked about important things like callings and dreams, it was like God Himself had crafted her in mind for me. She aligned with everything, said yes to everything, and sided with me in every passionate debate I had, even when she was at odds with her parents when I met them.

"What do you mean you're not having kids right away?" Her mom wrung her hands and weaved them through her brunette hair.

"He wants to wait a few years, and I support his decision. What is so wrong about that?" Jessica perched a hand on her hip.

"Well, your father and I didn't wait and we turned out fine

having all of you. I just think that you aren't trusting God enough, especially since you want to get married."

Man, our parents would get along great.

Despite their disagreement, she didn't buckle under her mother's argument. Leading up to the proposal today, my hands grew jittery as each hour passed. When we walked in the park together, my skin paled more than usual, as if an angel revealed himself while saying, "Don't be afraid."

You got this, Lincoln. She loves you. You love her. She trusts you, and you trust her.

We stopped for a moment on the bridge where I was gonna pop the question.

"Did I ever tell you that you make me incredibly happy?

"Really?" She wrinkled her nose at me. "What gave it away?"

"Well, the way you look at me, how you stand up for me, how you trust me. And to be honest. You took a chance on me, and I want to take a cha—"

Before I could finish, some kids ran through us on the bridge. I think they were playing tag. They rushed past her and nearly knocked her over. When they disappeared, I raced to her side.

"Are you okay?" I clasped her arm and assessed her for any injuries.

"Oh, I'm fine. Gosh, they're so adorable." She fluttered her hands and landed them on her chest, where her heart was. "I can't wait to immediately have my own kids with you." Then she clasped my arm and squeezed. Hard.

I stumbled back, almost wrenching out of her grip. *What does she mean by immediately?*

"Well, we have a few years until after the wedding to look into that." I crinkled a smile at her, coaxing her to remember her promise to me. What she'd said all those months ago.

"Well, we certainly don't know how the future will go,

even with planning." I noticed a bite in her tone. Almost like she was upset at being found out. She wasn't making eye contact with me now, either.

I paused, looking at her, confused, bewildered.

Then I sucked in a deep breath. "Okay, but we talked about this, that we would plan accordingly so we could learn to live together first."

As I looked, waiting for an answer, she pulled her eyes away while she took a heavy breath. "Lincoln, why are you so against this?"

My eyebrows narrowed. "Excuse me?"

"Lincoln..." She gasped for air as if the words had slipped away. "I want kids."

"Yeah, I know. So do I. I've never been against it. We've talked about this."

"No, I mean, I want kids *within* our first year."

Do promises mean nothing anymore? How long has this been going on? I staggered back, this time away from her touch. It no longer felt comforting to me.

"Jess. We talked about this."

"I know we did. It's just...I thought I could change your mind." She passed me a hurt look.

As if *I* had been the one to hurt her. To break the promises made.

A ringing echoed through my ears. Did I just hear her right? "Change my mind? After you promised me that this was okay for you? What else are you hiding from me? That you want to be a stay-at-home wife?"

She didn't speak for a moment. Her eyes liquified as her lips stumbled over her words. "I just didn't think you would want to be a Worship Pastor forever. That maybe you would change your mind and want to settle for a real job for our family."

My mind erupted. I could feel the veins pop on my hands, in my forehead. "You...you knew this was my calling."

"Babe, how many successful Worship Pastors do you know? How many of them are working at a thriving church?"

"So my calling to ministry needs to be an overly financially successful one, like some megachurch? Is that what successful ministry is to you?"

She pressed her hands together and placed them against her lips. "I'm saying be realistic." Niagara Falls tears poured out of her eyes. "I just...want to grow a family with you the same as my parents did...do you not love me enough to make a necessary sacrifice for the sake of having a family?"

Love her?

I thought I did. But maybe it wasn't her I was in love with...but the idea she'd fabricated for me. I found myself wondering how many other lies she told.

"I thought I was." I pulled out the ring box from my back pocket, flipping it open. She looked at it, disillusioned. Every feature sagged as if she despised the very idea of a future with me. "But I have a calling. And you knew that I did. And if I am sacrificing my calling to God for you on a promise that you broke, then who am I sacrificing for then?" I slammed the ring box shut.

"Lincoln, I—"

"We're done."

5

HOEDOWN

NOAH

Who knew the "Cupid Shuffle" would be quite the workout?

Noah gripped the stitches in his sides and puffed out a long breath when the song concluded. Students, bedecked in cowboy hats and overalls, clapped when the music finished.

Noah grinned at Em, who had a sheen of sweat that glossed her forehead.

"Sit?" The music transitioned to a slow song, and pairings coupled up. Girls draped their arms around the necks of their hopeful-husbands-to-be.

Harmony, who wore a pink tutu, drew her date closer by tugging on his arm. Call Noah crazy, but the date—who, for the life of him, he couldn't remember the name of—recoiled at the touch. He'd noticed Harmony's date lingering his stare on Em a second too long. The glare he passed Noah when Noah and Em danced a little too close to "Cotton Eye Joe" also didn't go unnoticed.

Maybe the guy didn't understand social cues.

Or maybe he's not as into Harmony as he's pretending to be.

Em wicked the sweat off her upper lip and panted. "Yeah, that may be a good idea."

"Actually." Harmony's date shoved his pink cowboy boots —a request of Harmony—between the two of them. He hooked a thumb over his shoulder. "I was thinking about grabbing Harmony a drink. Care to join me to get Noah one, Em?"

Goodness, for the last time, they weren't dating. He could grab his own darn drink. They'd had to clarify this to about three passersby, who had clapped him on the back and told him congrats for finally settling down with someone.

Em's eyebrows threaded together, but she shrugged. "Sure."

Noah would've joined her, except his throat threatened to choke him with thirst. He doubted he could keep up with their jaunty pace as they headed inside a nearby building.

"I—" Harmony blinked, and he couldn't tell if her expression read suspicious or if the setting sun had blinded her into a squint. "I might follow behind. See if they need help, erm, carrying the drinks."

She skipped away, still following at a decent distance. Noah guessed so the other two wouldn't turn around and notice her following them.

He still couldn't get a read on Em's roommate and had no intention to. As far as he knew, Harmony rotated her "aesthetic" every other week. She chose to dress up as a cowgirl in one, and who knew what she'd go for next? Maybe Sherlock in another one. The theater housed plenty of eclectic folks, but Harmony seemed to be a whole other variety of unique.

Noah parked on a picnic table bench nearby and scrolled through his phone. As he wiped the screen against his pants to get rid of the excess perspiration, he spotted a missed call.

From Sarah, the director of the local theater.

His heart skipped a beat. He'd sent her the sample scenes

he'd compiled—crafted from Lincoln and Dylan's stories (with their permission, of course)—an hour ago. How had she already read it?

Maybe she read the first page and decided it was hopeless.

Eyeing the building that Em had disappeared into, he figured it would take them a good five minutes to find the drinks and bring them back out. He found refuge in a quiet place, hundreds of meters away, where the bass no longer throbbed the ground.

Then he dialed Sarah.

She picked up on the third ring. "Hey...is that...'Take You Home with Me' I'm hearing?"

Noah whistled. "Dang, it's that loud?"

"Eh, I'm a country music fanatic. You could probably play two notes, and I can name that tune. It's bad. An addiction, really."

That did explain why, during drama warm-ups for summer camp, Sarah played a lot of Carrie Underwood and Luke Bryant.

"Anyway." Sarah drew out the word. "Any chance you can go somewhere quieter?"

Once again, Noah eyed the building Em had disappeared into. No sign of Em. He rattled a text to her to let her know where he'd gone and then headed in the direction of the library. About a minute later, he'd reached it and placed the phone on his ear.

"Hello? Are you there, Noah?"

"Sorry." He settled on the black benches outside of the building. "Campus hoedown, and it's a long way to get away from the noise."

"No worries. I'd figured that was it and decided to order my groceries in the meantime. I'm the multi-tasking queen."

Oof, speaking of, he had to stop by Aldi this week. And fill up his tank. Knowing how much remained in his bank account, it might be a toss-up between the two. Maybe he could convince one of his floormates to carpool.

During the school year, Noah worked at the theater as the house manager to earn a pittance stipend. It would, at least, cover the groceries for the rest of the semester. Gas? He'd figured it out later.

"So, cutting to the chase, I got your script."

His breath hitched. "And?"

"First, and take this as gently as possible, it wouldn't hurt to have an editor look it over. Just to trim some redundancies and cliches. And to make it sound more like how people talk."

Oof, that sucker-punched his gut. He'd run it through Grammarly about three times, but he should've anticipated this feedback. After all, all his theater directors had criticism to pair with any compliments they gave him on stage.

"It's that bad, huh?"

"Oh, Noah." She clicked her tongue. "It's not bad at all. I love the idea. Dating woes are a huge hot topic around these parts—especially considering we have so many colleges in the Indiana area where people are looking for their future spouses."

That ebbed the initial blow. Maybe he didn't have to think about completely switching his career. Five seconds ago, he was tempted to change majors this late into the game.

He wiped his sweaty forehead and cringed at the scent coming from his armpits. So much for that cheap, pine-scented deodorant he'd gotten at the store the other day.

"But I do have one other suggestion, Noah, if you're open to it. To make it stronger."

"What's that?" Now that he knew he wasn't an absolute failure, he'd be down for just about any edit.

He heard a breeze on the other line. Maybe she'd decided

to go for a walk. Knowing her, she'd head to the grocery store on the call to save time.

"So I've noticed that the first two scenes are from the perspective of guys, which is great! But as I'm sure you know, in theater, we have a hard time getting men to go out for plays. Any way we can make some of these females or gender-neutral?"

He winced.

Although, yes, dating mishaps happened to anyone, he couldn't deny certain nuances guys felt. The pressure to provide for a family—even if they chose to marry a spunky career woman. The agonizing anxiety that came with having to make the first move. Battling the trite comments of, "The worst she could say is no."

No, it could be far, far worse.

Hence why he avoided dating in college.

"Erm. Well, I don't know if I can personally write those since I'm not a girl. Doesn't seem fair."

"Maybe you could ask around. Bring a coauthor on? As long as you're prominently named to put the board at ease?"

Hmm, maybe. It wouldn't hurt to have multiple perspectives.

He could hit up Em with stories she'd heard from her matches. Or the females in the theater department. Heck, even Harmony had mentioned some harrowing stories on the way to the hoedown.

"But." He swallowed, and his leg bounced up and down. "You think it has promise?"

No sense in pursuing it if the theater would shut it down at the end of the process.

"Yeah, I do. I won't go into details since I just got to Aldi —" Ah, so she *was* heading to pick up her groceries. "But I have my fair share of bad dating experiences. In my opinion, it's an epidemic. So if you need any stories, I'd love to share."

He made a mental note to include one of Sarah's tales and signed off the call just in time for a skinny guy to charge toward the library. His blue cowboy hat sailed behind him as he gripped the wooden door to the library. Tugged. Locked. Throwing a wide-eyed glance over his shoulder, he then lasered his stare at Noah.

"You haven't seen a girl who's in a fringe jacket pass by here recently, right?"

Noah didn't know the guy's name, but he recognized him from a gen-ed psych class they had taken together. This student seldom raised his hand and, despite his tall stature, would slouch in his seat when the instructor picked a victim for a pop quiz.

"Erm, not here, no."

During the entirety of the phone call, no one swung by the library. Probably because the academic buildings were locked during certain hours of the week.

"Phew." He slumped against the brick wall. A trail of sweat followed him down to the concrete as he hid himself beside the bench and Noah's figure. "Finally shook her off."

"Bad date?"

The guy considered his words for a long handful of seconds. "Well, it's a long story, but let's just say girls can be stalkers too."

Noah sucked on his teeth and let out a hiss.

He'd been no stranger to stalkers. Freshmen who entered the theater department made their crushes and intentions known to him early on. And he always found himself in the same room as them, no matter the variety of his schedule. When one of them, last year, tracked his Delta flight home, he fought the urge to report her to Campus Safety.

But they would've laughed at me. Told me to man up and appreciate the compliment of a girl being interested.

Thank goodness she transferred to another school that

summer. But she still slid up on all his stories and tagged him in memes and videos at 2 a.m.

A pang of sympathy struck his gut.

"So, a stalker, huh?"

The guy snorted and shook his head. His smile didn't even reach halfway to his eyes. "Yeah, it's a long story."

☙ 6 ❧

UNDER SURVEILLANCE

MAX

Aryianna was in my history class last semester, which says a lot, given she had a *history* of controlling guys. We both enjoyed history, and she had a real interest in the Roman Empire. And here I thought that only applied to men. At least, that's what the internet and personal experience taught me. She had a particular interest in Julius Caesar, given his experienced betrayal after all that he did to maintain the Empire in the war against Gaul and Pompey.

I ran into her at the library and asked her about the midterm paper we had to write for class. What was a simple question led to a long talk about history. She appreciated ancient Roman history, and I enjoyed more of the Eastern Roman variety.

"Oh, come on, Constantine is overpraised." She tossed me what I deemed a playful eyeroll.

"Overpraised? The guy set the stage for Christianity becoming both legal and legitimate, not to mention the Nicaean Council that led to Trinitarian doctrine."

"Oh no, I completely agree." She smirked and crossed her arms.

Did I just spot a cute nose wrinkle?

"That said, Caesar did reduce slavery and opened up citizenship for more people. This probably affected Apostle Paul later on, given his argument of Roman citizenship in Acts 16."

I pondered this. "That's a pretty good point. Dang, I didn't even consider that one."

A question led to a conversation. A conversation led to a first date.

Our first date went great. We talked about our majors and our lives back home. While it was a simple coffee date, the butterflies were certainly there. When I asked if she would be open to a second outing, she immediately said yes and even set up the day, time, and location. At the time, it was a big surprise.

When we began talking more, she opened up about her life back home and the type of church community she grew up in.

"Wait, so your church looked down on you because you were single?"

She nodded, and blush crawled up her cheeks. "Marriage was put on a pedestal to the point where a young woman older than twenty-two was seen as old or 'past her prime.'"

"That's...wow. Did they not know how basic biology worked?"

"I don't want to go into much detail. To keep it short, the single guys at my church...really desire a young wife." She shuddered.

That is just...creepy.

"I am so sorry that you went through that. How awful." I passed her a sympathetic look.

"You think so?"

"Yes! This is some weird cult-like behavior you're describing. That's insane."

She smiled, sighing in relief. "I appreciate that. For some

reason, people think that I am lying or exaggerating. I literally was told this by a guy after a first date."

"I believe you, honestly." She blushed as I said this.

As the weeks passed, we spent a lot of time together. Aside from classes, she and I were practically linked arm-in-arm. Dorm floor event? We went together. Pickleball tournament? Together. Punk 'N Pie event? You guessed it: together. It was a great honeymoon phase. And that was the keyword: phase.

The red flags began slowly popping up when she was waiting for me after getting off of work...in my dorm room.

"How did you get in my dorm?" Besides some open house hours, girls couldn't swipe in or get past the front lobby monitors. There were back doors, but they required a key.

"Your room key. I hope you don't mind." She dug it out of her pocket and flashed it.

I mean, I kinda do mind. That's weird.

"Right, but...how did you get my room key?"

"I asked your roommate if I could borrow it since I left my book bag in the room."

I frowned, scanning my memories. "But you...you had your book bag when I dropped you off at class."

Ary gave a blank stare with a forced smile. "Well, I did leave it here."

An awkward silence arose between the two of us. I let it slide. *A fight isn't worth it.*

One would think that would be the end of it. That the situation was so awkward that she wouldn't try that again. But she dug in deeper when I came home after a weekend vacation with the family. What was supposed to be a cute ice cream date turned out to be a big red flag, as big as the Soviet flag planted by the Red Army on the Reichstag of Berlin toward the end of World War II.

"Looks like your trip went well with the family," she commented.

"Yeah! It was a great time. We did a lot." I had mentioned a trip to her, so I didn't immediately spot any warning signs.

"It looked like fun! I think the lake would have been my favorite."

I processed her words. "I'm sorry?" Did she say *looked*?

"The lake. Lake Superior, yeah? It's a personal favorite."

"I never told you I was going to Lake Superior." Granted, it was weird of me not to specify where I'd be going to someone as close as her. But it just hadn't crossed my mind to give those details.

She froze. "Oh...well, you said you were visiting family in Wisconsin, so I just assumed you went."

"My relatives live two hours away from the lake."

"Oh. Well, you know, word travels fast on social media."

"I went by myself...and I didn't post any photos."

Her lip began twitching as she looked to be trying to catch her breath. "I-I-I just know it's one of your favorite places and that..."

I opened up the settings app on my phone. "Ary?"

"Yeah? Wh-wh-what is it, love?"

"Did...did you take my phone and add your contact to track me?" I'd heard of some couples doing stuff like this, but that involved some verbal consent beforehand.

She froze again. *No way out of this one*. "Look, I only did it to make sure that you were safe."

"To make sure I was safe? I was with my family."

"Well, I just didn't want to worry. Also, you typically go AWOL when you visit home, where you hardly respond to my texts. What was I supposed to do?"

I inched back. She was becoming less attractive by the minute. "Babe, that is creepy. Seriously, that is a breach of privacy."

"Hey, if the government can do it through the Patriot Act, then so can I."

That's...that's not even the same thing. When I drove her home, there was an awkward silence, and I didn't respond to her messages for a while after that. I hoped this would maybe get her to back off and eventually apologize....Nope.

10:00 A.M.

> Ary: Hope your presentation goes well! Tell me how it goes.

10:30 a.m.

> Ary: So, how did your project go?? You must've knocked them dead!

10:45 a.m.

> Ary: Want to get coffee and lunch to talk about it? :)

11:30 a.m.

> Ary: Love, is everything okay? Are you still mad at me?

11:45 a.m.

> Ary: Wow, you're playing the silent treatment? Fine. Two can play at that game.

12:15 p.m.

> Ary: Baby, I'm sorry! Please respond! I miss you!

12:30 p.m.

Ary: ?!?!?!?!

This went on all day until I finally responded. It was as if I was kidnapped or dead and somehow miraculously returned. She gave me the most awkward, long, tight hug and kisses all over my face. It was weird!

The stalking didn't stop, by the way. On one hand, I just wanted her off my tracking app. On the other hand, how would I tell her? If I deleted her, I wouldn't hear the end of it. If I approached her, she would overly panic about where I would be at all times.

I decided to at least talk to Campus Safety about it. *Maybe they can help with stalkers.* I figured with Title IX in place, it would apply here. After I told Campus Safety my story, however, the officer just laughed. "Most men have a hard time getting women to even pay attention to them, bud."

I tried to explain how serious it was.

He rolled his eyes. "Look, pal, I have some actual emergencies to attend to. If you wouldn't mind, close your door on the way out."

Needless to say, I had no help.

And so I carried on. And I didn't stop to put two and two together until visiting her family for a family reunion last week.

During the visit, I met her three sisters. One had gotten engaged, the youngest was expecting her first kid, and the oldest was homeschooling all four of hers. I noticed how each sister was praised and congratulated on their "achievements." Her? It was pretty passive.

"She's graduating soon." The lights dimmed in her mother's eyes when she said this.

There was a smattering of halfhearted applause from everyone. My intestines twisted at the awkwardness.

"And who is this you brought today?" her older sister, Candice, asked.

"This is my boyfriend, Max."

"It's a pleasure to officially meet all of you." I shook her hand. She seemed put off by my gesture as she eyed me down, from my feet to my forehead.

"So, you finally landed one, did you?" The sneer was unmistakable.

Ary laughed off the embarrassment, as did I, but I could tell she was uncomfortable. Her laugh sounded forced.

I looked around the family room and saw how her family idolized marriage. Everyone in that room had a spouse. Heck, even the kids played house in the playroom where they were all married.

On the drive back to school the following day, I tried to bring it up with Ary.

"Do you mind if I ask something about your family?"

"What?" She crossed her arms, and her tone came out cold.

"Do your...do your sisters have a superiority complex?"

"Come again?"

"What I mean is, are they trying to one-up each other?"

"In what way?"

"In their relationships. I was just observing, and it seemed like that—"

"You're reading into things."

Awkward pause.

"Okay, I'm just asking because I noticed how you were uncomfortable—"

She blasted off her playlist connected to the speaker. Some purity culture Christian song about no dating until marriage.

"Babe, I was only asking because I just want to make sure that you are okay..."

Speakers got louder.

The conversation home was a disastrous one. For the next month, she would not-so subtly hint at engagement. If I tried to shrug off the conversation, she'd pout and shut down for the rest of the day.

It's been less than six months!

Not only was she stalking every movement on my phone, but she also would invite herself to various events and study sessions I attended. Even for the hoedown event just now. I was rehearsing for a number with our floor for the event, and she showed up unexpectedly.

"I thought you said that you had an exam to study for."

"Well, when you said you were going with your floor, I wanted to tag along."

"Right, but we're performing, and I'm not even staying after our performance due to studies. I told you this."

"Well, I just wanted to make sure that you were okay and that maybe we could have fun together."

I let out an exasperated breath. "Ary, why do you feel the need to attend everything with me?"

Her eyebrows threaded together as she tripped over her words. "I-I just thought that maybe we could make more memories together."

"But this performance is a guy's moment, and I wanted to spend it with just them." Sometimes, the hoedown hosted performances of certain floors, like the lip sync battle that happened later in the year. Most of the time, it was for group dances in general. But if she had her way, she'd be up there dancing with all the boys just to be close to me.

"Oh, so you want to leave me alone then?"

She liked to do this. Take any boundary and turn it against me. "I didn't say that; I said I want to be alone sometimes with other friends. Isn't that okay even for you?"

She stood in silence for a moment. "Is there someone else?"

"What?" I blinked a few times to make sure I heard right. What was with her catastrophizing everything?

"You're seeing someone else, aren't you?"

"How did you even come to that conclusion? No, I'm not seeing anyone else."

"Then let me come with you." She snatched my arm, gripping it as if we were one and the same. "I should be allowed to go with you."

"Babe, you're hurting my arm." I tried to release her without shoving or pushing her away. She only gripped tighter.

"Babe, please let me go with you!"

"All right, that's enough!" She dropped her grip. I had never raised my voice at her before.

I couldn't take it anymore. I also thought about her family situation. *Do I break it off, allowing her to continually be shamed by her family? Or do I let the stalking continue to where I propose and hope that God will bless our marriage?*

"Baby, please listen to me! I'm sorry I hurt you; I didn't mean to." Her fingers clawed at the air. Almost like she wanted to grab my arm again, but her brain short-circuited when she realized she couldn't.

"All I asked for was space to be with friends. I have given you every moment when I wasn't in class or at work. And then you criticize me for cheating when I just wanted to be with guys? We're through, Ary."

She didn't miss a beat, almost as if she hadn't heard me right. "Babe, you are under a lot of stress from this hoedown performance and the exam tomorrow. Please, let us talk this out."

"Ary, you're what's stressing me out. I get that your family is the way it is about marriage, but if this is what dating is like with you, then God help me if this is what marriage will be like."

I began walking away back to the guys, only for her to follow me. I quickly moved through the crowd as she trailed behind.

"Max!" she cried out as she pushed through the cowboy crowd. I managed to swiftly change cowboy hats on a rack to throw her off as I made my way through the back door.

Noah had paled a lot in the last few minutes. I hadn't realized how much it took to offload that.

"Sorry if I shared too much..."

Noah shook his head. "No, I get it, man. You have to talk to someone about that kind of stuff." He paused and dug out his phone. "I have a favor to ask. How would you like to get out your story again? This time, on paper."

7
MONSTERS
NOAH

"I don't know if this pink paint is reading 'scary' enough." Noah frowned at the polka dots he'd freckled the paper with. With what spare time he had left, he'd volunteered to help his dorm decorate for their open house. This year, it was themed after the famed *Monsters, Inc.* movies.

"But we're calling it Scary Monsters." Their RA had shrugged, holding a clipboard in the middle of the hallway earlier that day. "Don't want to risk any copyright issues."

A professional writing student by the name of Chuck, a short guy with a short haircut and a long, baggy hoodie observed the mural Noah painted of two monsters roaring at a scared college student.

"Dude." Chuck chuckled. "I thought you helped out with painting sets and stuff. What's up with the Pepto Bismol pink?'

True, Noah did volunteer in several positions in the theater. Their classes required them to hone their skills on and off the stage. Yet, despite having painted sets in the past, he'd much rather land as a technical director or house manager at a nearby theater than have to draw one more ivy vine or brick out of paint.

Maybe I'll land an actor or director position if I'm lucky.

That wouldn't happen for years, though. Even when he'd joined the major, he knew the odds.

Noah smirked and smeared his hand against his forehead. It took him a second to realize he'd glossed a sheen of paint onto his skin. Sure enough, a blotch of it soiled his fingers and knuckles.

"Wanna lend me a hand, then, Chuck? Since I'm not the greatest at this stuff?"

"Listen, I'm an editor at heart when it comes to the written word." Chuck thumped his chest. "But I don't think I'm an editor when it comes to painting. I can't exactly erase that and 'type over it.'"

Fair enough.

Noah's ears perked at the mention of the word editor. Though his theater schedule didn't allow him to touch his play for Sarah much, he did manage to gather a few stories from the women at the theater. Perhaps he could hit up Em soon if Em didn't keep going on terrible dates that ruined the rest of her day.

We haven't been able to talk as much this year.

But she'd go to the open house tonight, so at least they had that to look forward to. Noah noticed how his days sombered without her. Had a little less spark.

Chuck crouched and spattered some scarlet paint on the white poster board, like blood droplets.

"Whoa." Noah held up his hands. "I think our RA said to keep this PG."

Chuck grimaced. "Whoops." He set the paint can down and reached for another tray, one with sky-blue hues inside. "Guess I wasn't able to listen to the whole speech he gave."

That was right. Chuck had ducked out to field a phone call from his girlfriend.

Noah didn't know much about her. Other than the fact that her hair coiled in perfect ringlets, like the wires on old phones. And that she often insisted he go to her dorm and not the other way around. He doubted she'd grace them with her presence tonight.

"You didn't miss much. Mostly, we're doing a *Monsters, Inc.* theme but for college students. So all the scary things we go through from DTRs to failed grades, you get the point."

"Sounds fun." Chuck's phone buzzed again, and he groaned.

"Hey." Noah dipped his brush into a nearby murky water cup. Paint fumes sent him into a dizzy frenzy. He stood and stepped away. Best to get some air until his brain stopped pounding. "You do edits from time to time for a fee, right?"

Noah had stepped in as a house manager for a recent opera at the school, so that earned him a stipend that could *hopefully* cover those expenses. Because of this addition to a busy schedule, he hadn't touched the play in a bit.

No use in sending it out if it needs some cleanup.

"Yeah, since I haven't graduated yet, my rates are pretty dirt-cheap. What are we thinking?"

Noah explained the premise of the play, and Chuck tensed.

His eyes widened. Most of the time, Noah received appreciative nods from the guys when he explained the mission and message of the show. Had he somehow missed the mark?

"Erm. Everyone's kept anonymous. Your name wouldn't go on it if you edited it. Unless you want—"

Chuck shook his head. "It's not that. I think what you're doing is cool, man, but." He motioned to his pocket. Through the fabric, a phone glowed. It buzzed again. "I have a feeling she'd hate it if I was part of that."

Noah blinked once, twice. "Why? You'd just be editing it. It's not like we're including your story. Besides, we've had girls contribute to the play, too, so we're showing that all sexes are equally terrible to each other—if your girlfriend is worried about if it's a play that's just trashing women."

Chuck planted his hands on his hips.

"It's not even that. She's..." He scanned the water-stained ceiling, perhaps for the right words. As an editor, he'd have to pick them well. "She's one of those people who gets annoyed when single people complain about dating stuff."

"Why?" Especially if she was dating someone, why would she care?

"I don't know. Thinks they're doing something wrong or that they somehow earned it? I try not to ask questions. She, erm." His brown eyes crinkled. "Has a short fuse. And has made it clear that she has to win every fight."

Got it.

Noah didn't press the subject further. Chuck apologized and fled the scene, rushing to the elevator on their floor. Assuming Chuck would beeline to his girlfriend's dorm, Noah returned to his painting now that the paint-fume headache had gone away.

Chuck didn't return for most of the open house, but he'd drifted from Noah's mind when Em arrived. They split gummy-worm cupcakes and explored the various "scare" rooms. Em had "scared" Jeff, a volunteer for the event, in the DTR room. The story was really funny when she told it.

Warmth filled Noah's chest at their interactions.

Yes, she plagued him with questions about Jeff. No doubt, she'd secured her next "match" for her business. But for some reason, Em made the time disappear. And of all the girls on campus, she was the only one not scary enough to talk to.

At least in the sense that she wouldn't try to force him to date her.

Noah had learned early on that most theater girls equated stage kisses with actual advances. They'd string him along with the prospect of a friendship, only to tell him, three months in, that he better ask them out or step out of their lives.

I don't know why Chuck's girlfriend is so mean to single people. We have it just as hard as the couples do.

When Em stepped onto the elevator to leave, a figure in a yeti costume rushed out of the sliding doors. The onesie stunk of musk, and Noah wondered if the student had somehow picked it up from a thrift store.

The person threw off the yeti mask and revealed a panting Chuck inside. "Did I miss it? I've been trying to get back for hours, but—" He didn't finish. Didn't have to.

Chuck's girlfriend bent time and space itself, turning five minutes into five hours. Noah had a feeling that she ate his time—rather than fulfilled it. Em, on the other hand, somehow made time with Noah feel like a worthy investment.

I guess those closest to us take our time away from us. But what they did with it made all the difference. Some gave back double in good memories. Others vacuumed people dry until they had no hopes, no dreams, nothing left.

"Erm." Noah checked his phone. "We might have about fifteen minutes left. Want to help the guys out in the Deadline room? They can use a few more wailing, insomniac monsters in there."

"Sure, that sounds—argh!" A vibrating phone punctuated his exclamation. He smeared a hand down his face as he checked his device. "You've gotta be kidding me."

"Maybe put the thing on Do Not Disturb?"

Chuck let out a cold laugh. "Good luck with that. Tried that, and she figured out all the ways to bypass it. Asked if I was ignoring her and seeing other girls. She monitors my locations like it's her job."

That sounds...unhealthy.

Noah licked the vanilla frosting off another cupcake and crumpled the wrapper, pitching it at a garbage can.

For the second time that day, third, if he counted the RA meeting in the hallway, Chuck disappeared.

And that *is why I don't date people on campus.*

He imagined anyone would tell him he couldn't go out for certain roles. Even if he faked the kisses on stage or let the girlfriend watch rehearsals, that jealousy would spike. Or they'd get envious of his time spent at the theater anyway and would make him pick a different career path, one with more consistent hours.

As the open house drew to a close, Noah picked off streamers that hung from the ceiling. When he jumped up to reach one stuck in a ceiling tile, the elevator door dinged.

A figure with bunched fists and a scrunched neck like a coat hanger stormed out.

Chuck rounded the corner, past the ping-pong table in the common area, and charged toward Noah.

"You." Chuck softened his voice and expression, perhaps catching onto the intimidating demeanor of both. "I want to be part of your play."

"On the edits?" Noah felt himself brighten. "That's great, man, I—"

"Not just the edits, although...I can help out with that. For free, too."

Oh, shoot. Noah would at least bargain with him to let him pay for Chuck's lunch at TSC sometime.

"I'll edit it for free...if you let me include a story in it. Mine."

Dread pooled in Noah's stomach. Something had gone down in the last hour; it had to have.

"Oh, yeah, we can do that. But won't your girlfriend be a little hesitant if you included a story about her...or maybe one of your exes?" He did remember how some girls on campus would bristle when someone mentioned an old flame, even in negative terms.

"Ex-girlfriend—"

Dang.

"—and trust me, I don't care if I'm anonymous or not."

8
SO THIS IS LOVE?
CHUCK

Catherine was...something. We met only a month ago in our English literature class. I should have seen the red flags, given that she was obsessed with Jane Austen. I loved the 2020 Netflix adaptation of *Emma* and enjoyed the 2005 film adaptation of *Pride and Prejudice*. Matthew McFayden was brilliant.

While I loved those stories, Catherine, however, was obsessed with them and wouldn't stop talking or quoting them. I am not against a love for books since I have read Dante's *Divine Comedy* multiple times. Heck, my priest can recite it in the original Italian. It's one thing to be a fan of someone's work. It's another when it transforms into an unhealthy lifestyle.

I say this because we bonded over those books when we read them for class. When we were in the same study group, she practically led every session.

"Wow, you know a lot about Jane Austen's work," I noted.

"Thanks!" She blushed. "She's been my favorite since I was a kid. My family read the books every year growing up."

"Dang, that's cool. This is my first time reading them."

"You've never read them before??" Her eyes widened.

I was taken aback by her shock. "I mean, I saw the movies, which were great."

"Oh, the books are so much better! You'll love them!"

I'm gonna be honest: I was attracted to her love for them originally. It's quite attractive when someone has a love or a fondness for any hobby or craft. After our project had finished, I decided to make a move.

"I think we did well in that group presentation!" she said as we walked out of class together.

"Well, we did have a very knowledgeable leader." I smirked. She flushed. We waved goodbye to the other group members. They rolled their eyes after noticing us.

As we headed toward the student center, we both stopped to part ways. "Well, I best be getting to my next class then." She hooked a thumb over her shoulder.

"Yeah, for sure. I got work in a bit." We had a cute silence together as we both turned pink. We spent the next few seconds communicating words via our eyes.

"Okay, well, I should go." She started to pad away.

I was still frozen. As if the sun was melting the ice off my legs, I slowly began moving toward her nervously. "Hey."

She whipped around with a hopeful smile. "Yeah?"

"Umm..." My face burned red as I stared at the ground. "I, uhhh...like you." It was nearly spoken as a whisper. "I think you're great, and you're cute when you talk about books, and I was hoping if you would like to—"

She grabbed my jacket and pulled me in for a kiss. I numbed as I tried to grasp what was happening. "...yeah, I would like that." She pulled away, nodded, and flashed a quick smile.

"Wow, uhhh...o-o-okay. I'll uhhh...text you?" My body shivered as it attempted to regain composure.

"I'll respond when you do." She winked. As she darted

away, I stood there confused, like a lost freshman on their first day of class.

Did that...did that just happen?

Our first date was Saturday of the same week, where we spent nearly the entire day together. Our first stop was at the Covered Bridge Festival, followed by the Billie Creek Village. With it being the fall season, we got into typical fall attire. Flannels, scarves, you name it.

When we arrived, the bright orange trees blocked the sunlight, while fallen leaves blanketed the streets and trails. Talk about a Hallmark movie moment. We took a ride on the Zombie Hayride, which spooked her. Due to her brother's love for *The Walking Dead* growing up, she was terrified of them and held onto my arm the entire time. Afterward, we went under the 1906 Beeson Bridge, where she clung to me as if she were on the edge of a cliff. Afterward, we grabbed ice cream and matchas from the local coffee shop. From there, we stopped under the newly painted gazebo in the village.

"I can't get enough of matchas, honestly." She nearly downed her drink in one gulp.

"My Ohio cousin loves these. She took me to her favorite coffee shop called Evelyn's, in Akron over the summer. After my first sip, I immediately fell in love with them."

"That's not the only thing I'm immediately falling for today." She kissed me on the cheek. I blushed as we both stared at each other. "Uh, Chuck?"

"Y-y-yeah?" I had gotten lost in her stare.

"Your ice cream's melting."

I immediately cleaned my hand off as the sticky raspberry flavor dripped off my index finger. She giggled.

"Sorry, I've just...I've never really had good first dates before, and I've been nervous."

"No, it's okay. Same with me."

"Really?" My eyes narrowed. *A pretty girl like her?*

"Yeah. I weirded out guys too much."

"Well, they must be the weird ones then."

She grabbed my hand as we leaned in for a kiss.

Is this a dream? Someone tell me this is a dream.

When we got back to her dorm, we decided to watch *Pride and Prejudice* in the dorm lounge since it was after-hours. One of her floormates passed by on her way in.

"Is that *Pride and Prejudice*?" Her floormate lit up. Maybe she loved Austen as much as Catherine.

"Yup." I checked my watch. "It just started, like, five minutes ago."

"Nice. I have yet to see it."

"You can come watch with us if you'd like." I patted an open chair next to the couch Catherine and I were sitting on.

"You sure? If so, I'll get my blanket."

"Sorry," Catherine threw a withering glare at me. "But this is just for us two."

"Oh." I frowned. Catherine's tone had never gotten that icy before. "I mean, it's okay with me if she wants to."

"It's our first date, love." She flashed fiery eye contact at the other girl. "I'd like to keep it that way."

An awkward silence echoed in the lobby. "All righty then." The other girl shrugged and disappeared into the stairwell.

Catherine pulled me in closer as she rested her head on my shoulder. I honestly didn't know what to do. We were having a great first date, and I didn't want to ruin it. While I brushed it off for the most part, the awkwardness from a few moments ago still lingered.

After the movie ended, she walked me out of her dorm, holding my hand tight. "Hey, I had a good time. You made today special." Her cheery smile made me melt again.

"I'm glad I could." My face and neck felt warm.

"So, I'll see you tomorrow after church?"

"Yeah, of course. I'll see you tomorrow."

She kissed me on the cheek and headed back to her dorm building. I returned to my dorm and passed through the lobby. Normally, it was empty on a Friday night, but some of my bros had stayed behind to hear the details.

"Hey, man," Clark said, "how did your first date go?"

"Yeah, bro!" Bruce slapped me on the back. "What's the story? What's her name?"

"It uhhh...it went great." I winced. How did guys normally talk about this stuff? Lots of details or simple?

"That's....that it?" Clark frowned. "You seemed all in on this girl before you left."

"No, don't get me wrong, it was a great date." I tossed up my hands. "But something threw me off toward the end that was weird."

"What happened?" Bruce pulled up a chair. I went for a glass of water from the water filter in the kitchen lounge.

"Most of it was great. We went to the village in fall season attire."

"Very nice." Clark elbowed Bruce in the gut and winked.

"And then took a lot of photos on a trail, did the Zombie Hayride, and had a great lunch. I mean, she's really into me."

"Sounds like a keeper." Bruce poured himself some hot coffee from his pour-over. "So what's the problem then?"

I recalled what had happened in the lobby when the other girl had asked to see the movie with us.

"What did she say?" asked Clark.

"Her floormate asked if she could join in watching, and she immediately told her off and that it was only for the two of us. I was fine with her joining, but she insisted." I drank another sip of water.

"Wait." Bruce went for a third gulp of coffee. He called his "detective juice" since he was majoring in Criminology. "Does she live in Alpha?"

"Yeah," I cocked my head, "how did you know?"

"Does she have an obsession with Jane Austen?"

My eyebrows drew together. I didn't like where this was going. "I would call it more of a deep passion, but yeah, Jane Austen nonetheless."

"Mmmmm, is her name Catherine?" Bruce grimaced. Something in his tone told me he hoped he was wrong.

I hoped he was, too. "Yeah, that's her."

He let out a deep breath. "...so Chuck." He put his hand on my shoulder. "I am gonna say this as delicately as I can." His tone came out sincere. I've never known him to be anything but. "Catherine...can be clingy."

"Okay?" I waited for the punchline. Lots of girls on campus could be.

"No, I mean *clingy*." Bruce took his hand off my shoulder. "She dated my ex-roommate Rob last semester, and he dropped her immediately."

Yeah, but Rob was a picky guy. We all knew that about him. "Why? Anyone can be clingy in the honeymoon phase, let alone the first few dates."

"She's not just clingy physically; she's clingy in everything. She plans for everything, everywhere, all at once to where she even has backup plans."

I playfully laughed. "Wouldn't that just be efficient? That sounds like a Type-A person."

Bruce took a breath, bringing his hands together before his face. "Okay, you're not hearing me. She plans for everything, and I mean *everything*."

"Uh-huh." I frowned again, waiting for another punchline. "Look, as weird as that moment was with her, I do want to give her the benefit of the doubt. Maybe it was a misunderstanding. I'll bring it up tomorrow with her over lunch."

Clark and Bruce exchanged eyebrow raises. Bruce spoke. "Okay. You can do that, by all means. Though I think if you bring it up, you'll see what we mean."

"Right." An uncomfortable silence squeezed my gut. For a split second, I'd wondered if they were right. "Well, I'm gonna catch up on some sleep." I slowly walked away as they talked amongst themselves.

"He's in for a rude awakening," I heard them say.

Okay, that moment may have been an odd one, but one odd moment doesn't describe an entire person's character.

After I got out of the Latin Mass that morning at St. Margaret's Church, I headed to Catherine's dorm to pick her up. By this point, I'd shaken off the conversation I'd had with the guys.

"Hey, you." I beamed at her. "How was your morning?"

She didn't return my pleasant look. "You were supposed to be here fifteen minutes ago." She folded her arms.

I playfully laughed. It took me a moment to absorb her body language. "Oh, you're serious."

"Yeah, I am."

"Well, today was the Latin Mass, and Fr. Hayden chants nearly every part of the liturgy, which goes a little longer." That was my favorite, by the way. I thought I'd told her about this before, but maybe I'd forgotten to. It didn't seem like a big deal.

"When you say you're gonna be here at a specific time, make it at that time."

Being caught off guard, I shifted topics quickly. I had a few autistic friends who were pretty big on people showing up on time. Maybe she was a little like that. "Okay, so where shall we go for lunch then?"

She opened up her calendar book.

Do people still use those?

As she flipped through it, my blood went cold. Everything I saw was specifically planned out. *Oh, shoot, Bruce and Clark weren't kidding!* To make it even worse, she had a bunch of hearts around my name on future calendar dates.

"Uhh, what are those heart dates?" Sweat brimmed on my upper lip.

"Oh, those are our future dates that I planned out." She passed me an eager smile and a wide-eyed gaze as if this was just normal people behavior.

My eyelids crinkled as if trying to decide whether she was serious or not. "But we haven't even discussed when a third date would be."

"Yeah, that's why I said *I* planned it out." There was a bite to her voice.

"Right, but what if these dates conflict with classes or work?"

"I already planned around those." She began writing in her calendar.

"Oh."

Panic welled in my throat, but I choked it down.

"Yeah. I always have a backup plan for everything." She flipped through a few pages.

Did she...oh gosh.

"I'm sorry, but did I just see that you planned our engagement?"

This went way beyond autistic at this point. I knew some autistic folks on campus. Emerson, that matchmaking girl, was one of them. Even if she was an organized person, she wasn't this fanatical.

"Well, we're dating, Chuck," Catherine rolled her eyes, "we have to plan ahead."

"Catherine, don't you think that's a bit much? *'A bit' is putting it lightly.*

She stopped writing and stared ahead. She sucked in a slow, deep breath as if holding in her anger. "Baby, back when times were simpler, people planned for this, especially women, given how they needed to raise families early and quickly."

Oh gosh, is this a nightmare? Someone tell me this is a nightmare. This can't be real! My surroundings started to suffocate me. "I'm sorry, you're already talking about kids?"

"I'm sorry," she snapped back, "don't you want to be a father someday?"

"Yeah, *someday*. Not before a second date." I pinched the bridge of my nose. I could not believe we were having this conversation.

"Wow. I can't believe we're having this discussion right now."

Uh, same here!

She sighed deeply, cooling off. "Look, it hasn't been an easy morning." Her bottom lip sunk into a pout. "We got a B on our Jane Austen project."

"Okay?" I frowned. That alone shouldn't have caused her to plan an entire future with someone she barely knew. "That's still a passing grade."

Blood drained from her face. "Still a passing grade? I know Jane Austen better than the professor does! I did all the research because I know all the research. And she gave me a B?" She folded her arms again, tight as tree roots knotted together. "You know, if you read the book, maybe we would've gotten an A on the project, Mr. I-Just-Watch-the-Movies."

We drove off to our second date, brunch. In the midst of it all, at least real food was involved compared to the college cafeteria, the same cafeteria that had caterpillars in the salad and green eggs (not the Dr. Seuss kind).

But my appetite went sour when we arrived at brunch, where her parents were waiting for us. For the next hour-and-a-half, I was grilled on marriage "trivia" as Catherine talked endlessly about our upcoming dates, engagement rings, and even wedding dresses. *Freaking. Wedding. Dresses!*

Nearly every moment of free time was eaten up by her. If

it was a double date, it would be with her friends, not mine. If I wanted to hang out with the guys, even for floor events, she ranted about how much she "sacrificed" for our relationship by planning our future, a future that I had no say in.

Bruce and Clark became increasingly concerned. "You need to confront her, man." I had never pulled the trigger on ending a relationship before, so I kept putting it off until tonight.

In between when I left and returned, she confronted me. "You've been helping your floor so much that I barely see you anymore."

After nearly a month and a half of this, I couldn't take it.

"With all due respect, Catherine..."

"Uh, love, I'm 'babe' to you."

"Can you please let me say my piece for once?"

She looked stone cold. I could tell no one had ever spoken to her like that before. Not even her parents.

Still, I forged on. I had to.

"You have a lot of nerve to tell me I am not putting enough into this relationship. For weeks, I have done nothing but give up every spare moment to you, bowing down to your every demand, request, and plea. I have shut my mouth when I have wanted to disagree with you, knowing that if I already made plans, you would play the emotional card."

She had a look of dismay as she smacked her teeth. Her eye contact drew away as if gazing off elsewhere would lower my volume.

By now, I'd learned all her tricks. It wouldn't work. *Not again.*

"I am tired. I am tired of you controlling my schedule. I am tired of you controlling my friends. And I am tired of you controlling my life and my future."

She shot back a scathing look. "Well, if that's how you feel."

"Yeah, it is. We're done."

"Fine." She began storming away down the hall. She stared me down one last time. "You could've been the Darby to my Elizabeth."

My eyes narrowed. "Don't you mean Darcy?"

She gaped for a moment, huffed, and spun around.

And just like that, she was gone.

Finally.

9
A HAPPY STORY
NOAH

"Hey, Noah."

One of the female theater freshmen loomed over Noah in the hair and makeup room for the theater department. Hot lights in front of the mirrors formed perspiration on Noah's lips.

Should've anticipated this.

That the understudy for the girl who kissed him in *Matchmaker* would mistake his friendliness for advances. Some of his friends said he sounded flirty in his interactions, and he didn't mean to. He had no idea how to turn that off, even when he purposely drained his voice of all color to drop hints. At a Christian college like this, anything could've been mistaken for flirtation. When people were desperate enough to find their "kingdom spouse," every minor change in the expression could look like a clue...

"Hey, erm." He couldn't remember her name. "You. Any chance you've seen my makeup foundation? Can't find it anywhere."

She bounced away from his seat and raced to the cabinets

that were situated right in front of the costume room. That would keep her occupied for a few minutes as she scavenged for his Ben Nye palette. Every student had their own set of makeup the theater provided.

"Don't bother with him." The lead of the play, Gwen, fiddled with her red wig and winked at Noah. "He's not planning on dating anyone while at college. A fact that." She lifted a finger. "I admire him for. Makes things easier."

Gwen had toyed with the idea of Noah for about two seconds when they paired off for a ten-minute scene during their first year at Mansfield. She'd moved on to another guy soon after that. Then dropped dating altogether after a heartbreak or two.

The freshman girl stationed at the makeup cabinet huffed and stalked off.

Noah chuckled and leaned toward Gwen. "Reminds me of when guys hold doors for girls just so they can get a date with them." It still blew his mind that some guys did that. Ruined it for the rest of them when they just wanted to be polite. Noah had been told off more than once by a girl on campus that she "wasn't interested" when he held open the library doors for her.

Gwen rolled her eyes before gooping some old mascara onto her lashes. Yeesh, the theater department needed to invest in more up-to-date cosmetics. "Yeah, no one does anything nice just for the sake of it."

No wonder their director had started a "Do Good" initiative for *Matchmaker.* They could encourage students and teachers to complete altruistic acts, not expecting payment in return.

It's a Christian school. You'd think that if anyone understood servant-leadership, it would be us. Quid pro quo things made no sense to someone like him. Someone who grew up confused by why people would mooch off his parents and act nice around them just to get a handout.

"It's why I don't trust anything free." He stood to search the makeup cabinet for his foundation. He found it at the bottom of a plastic bin. His name, Noah, on the clouded lid, had almost smeared off. "Any offer of coffee? Any compliment...it's always loaded."

Gwen smirked as she streaked on deep red lipstick, one to match her wig. "Hence why I stopped dating after a couple of guys. It's been so freeing. I see why you do it. Not date girls in your case, I mean."

Before Noah could respond, a familiar silhouette marched into the costume room. He had to double-take and inch his way to the doorway to check. Sure enough, next to a tenor doing vocal warmups by ball gown racks, Sarah rifled through the clothes on another Z-rack.

"Sarah?"

She peeked between the tulle of two gowns and beamed at him. "Hey! I didn't know you were in tonight's play. Although, I should've guessed. I hear you lead in all their productions."

He laughed as he made his way over to her. His feet dodged sewing needles that littered the linoleum floor. "Did you get lost on your way to the bathroom or something?" Theater patrons sometimes accidentally stumbled into the makeup room on their way to the restrooms.

Sarah pursed her lips and shook her head.

"Nah." Metal hangers flickered through her sharp nails. "I've been meaning to pick up some stuff for *Sense and Sensibility* for our theater, and your director said to come in anytime. We share supplies. I'm sure you know by now that that's a frequent thing theaters do."

Good to know that theaters in the area networked.

Maybe by May, something could open up where he didn't have to venture deep into a rat-infested apartment in a large city. Past actors from the program had returned to give talks about their time in NYC or trying to break into the LA scene. Many shared apartments with multiple people—making dorm living out to be some kind of luxury. Some loved it. But considering Noah endured the conditions of his dorm for four years, he didn't want to venture back into that kind of living space for a while.

The thought of finances reminded him of something else, something that had twisted his gut for weeks.

He needed to get started on a GoFundMe for Em. If he could somehow collect twenty thousand dollars by the end of this year, maybe she'd give up this miserable bet with her apartment nemesis Jana.

Considering his family wouldn't scrounge up the money to get tickets to his plays when they happened to be in town—or the fact that his classmates wouldn't even go to the theater on a student discount...

He doubted his network would help much. Better to start early and harass his contacts until people gave in. Noah had watched a few students studying Christian Ministries do that. When they'd gotten an internship with certain ministries, they had to raise their salary for the year. They'd set up dinner meetings and phone calls with anyone they could. Most people would dodge them during that period of time. And he imagined he'd have a similar outcome.

As Noah doubled back to the dressing room to grab his phone, Sarah's voice halted him.

"Hey! Now that I have you, can I run something by you? Figured it's easier to do it here instead of on the phone."

He turned around, suddenly forgetting what he was about to do. *Oh well*, he'd remember it later. Leaning his shoulder against the door frame, he wrinkled his nose at the hairspray fumes that clogged and clouded the area.

"Sure, what can I help with?"

"First of all, I got the edited copies of your first scenes. Great job. And I'm happy to see some female perspectives in there, too." Sarah jiggled her shoulders. Sarah sometimes did that when she was happy. Or had an itch on her shoulders she couldn't reach.

Chuck had finished his edits this past week, and Noah had transcribed a few interviews from the females in the theater department. Noah decided to have the female scenes as monologues, using their exact words, cutting nothing out. That way, he couldn't intrude with his masculinity. Any director who spearheaded the production could choose as to whether they'd hire additional actors to act out the monologues—like a pantomime.

"I still think I may swap the gender of a few stories just because there are a few universal themes going on." Sarah tapped a thoughtful finger on her lips. "But that may come down to casting, too. Dynamics shift depending on who you choose, you know?"

Although he didn't warm up to the idea of major changes, he acquiesced. After all, Sarah had opened this opportunity for him. Surely, he could adjust wording here and there.

"But I do have one more favor I need to ask of you."

Noah grimaced. He'd started to hate looking at those scripts. Scanned them a million times, winnowing them for bad grammar and repeated words.

If she makes me rewrite the whole thing, I might quit on the spot.

"Nothing bad." Sarah held up her hands, a placating gesture. "I'm noticing that pretty much all of these stories are negative. Which granted." She motioned around herself. "In a place like this, where there's heavy pressure to get married right away, that's bound to happen. But works of literature are all about balance."

"Balance?"

"Yeah!"

She unfurled a play program from *Matchmaker.* That set him at ease, that she was here to do more than pick up costumes but to support his cast as well. It made it all the more special when artist folks helped one another.

"So I've seen *Matchmaker* before. Yeah, it's mostly funny, but there are a few somber moments. We see the opposite in your play. All sad, a couple of funny things—but nothing uplifting. We need that hope. It's a powerful tool."

"Okay...so you're saying you need more happy stories?"

She tapped her nose like the *ding-ding-ding* of a game show buzzer.

"Like, one or two, if we're looking at roughly ten scenes or stories. Maybe three if you're planning to have more than that. Just a few palate cleansers to help the audience shake off the heavy stuff."

Can't argue against that.

Once, his college theater director attempted to put on a play that was so sad a chunk of the audience walked out at intermission. People could only handle so much darkness.

Once he emerged from the dressing room, Noah cupped his hands over his mouth. When he spoke, everyone halted. "Does anyone have a 'good date' story? That they would feel comfortable with if I put it in a play?"

No one spoke for a moment.

Then, Gwen cinched her hand around the wrist of a scrawny junior and lifted his hand. "We do."

Noah squinted at her. "I thought that you two broke up."

They exchanged a shrug and a hearty laugh. Gwen wiped away a happy tear in her waterline and brushed the wrinkles out of her scarlet, plumed skirt.

"I mean, we did. We decided it wasn't the best fit, and we parted ways. But the dates were still good, wouldn't you say?" Gwen released the guy's wrist, and he nodded. A sheepish smile spilled onto his face.

Something told Noah that the man liked Gwen a lot more than she'd let on, perhaps even still. She couldn't reciprocate in the same fashion and did him a mercy by cutting it off.

"Mm." Noah grimaced. "I'm not sure if that counts. Let me check."

He bustled back into the dressing room as Sarah heaved gowns off the rack and chucked them onto a chair by a sewing machine.

"Back already?" She puffed out a breath and cinched her hands on her sides, perhaps to stop the stitches that had formed from her heavy labor.

"So when you say 'happy,' does that mean the couple has to end up together? What about people who parted ways but stayed friends?"

"Noah, dating is complicated. If you walked away from it without somehow getting hurt, I'd call that a win."

"So it counts?" Elation buoyed his chest.

"Sure." She wagged a finger at him. "I'd still like a happy ever after from one of the stories, though—"

Noted. He'd have to scavenge the campus for a success story. Perhaps, *ugh*, hit up one of Em's past clients. She did have a lot of good testimonials. He had to give her that. She was a good businesswoman. And unlike his parents, at least she tended to operate with integrity.

"—but I like the idea of platonic friends. Shows that love stretches more than one way."

"You got it!" Noah saluted her and charged back into the dressing room. By now, Gwen had disappeared, probably for a mic check. She'd left behind the scrawny boy, the ex-and-now-a-good-friend, in her wake. Noah cleared his throat. "Any chance that you're willing to tell me that story? The one about you and Gwen."

Gwen struck him as the chattier one of the pair, but the boy smiled and nodded.

"She was the one who got away, but honestly, I think I'm okay with it."

10

BEST FIRST/LAST DATE

JASON

You know, when it comes to potential relationships ending after a first date, it's typically due to red flags: rude behavior, opposite beliefs, or actions that are just plain creepy. With Gwen, however, she was a green flag, one hundred percent. We met in our Monsters and Mythology class (yes, that is a real course), a class dedicated to literature and history's deadliest and creepiest monsters. The one that she enjoyed was the great Cthulhu from H.P. Lovecraft.

"You like Cthulhu?" I asked.

"It's not even a contest when he is mentioned. Just look at his size!"

"I prefer Jörmungandr from Norse mythology." I smiled.

"*God of War* fan?"

I gave her a smile that said it all. "You know it."

She and I could talk about mythology all day, from hundreds of years ago to the most recent of stories. And it's because of that, along with a number of separate reasons, that I fell head over heels for her.

"Honestly, for my money, I think Ra could wipe him out." She passed me a coy smile.

"A sun god versus a god killer? Highly unlikely."

"Ra was on the brink of destroying all of humanity."

"And Jörmungandr killed the gods, Thor included."

"And died in the process at Thor's hand." She raised an eyebrow at me.

"Point still stands."

"Well, at the end of the day, none of them willingly die for humanity by being wrongfully condemned only to rise again, thus creating a path toward salvation."

"Whaaaaat? You mean mythological deities aren't superior to Christ the God-Man?"

She laughed. Not having much to do with my sarcasm, but hey, it was cute when she did.

By this point in our friendship, I had thought about possible first dates. I wasn't really big on "get-to-know-you" coffee dates. I found those boring. Forced conversation like that felt more like a job interview. Besides, I figured doing something we both liked would be better.

I couldn't think of anything until I saw an ad online: the mythology exhibit at the local history museum. Not just any mythology museum of one subject, but one of many. Egyptian, Greco-Roman, Norse, Native American, and even Japanese. It was a limited-time event, and it was right in the middle of fall break. It was perfect!

After class, I walked up to her, heart pounding, of course. *Get it together, Jason.*

"Hey, Jason. What's up?"

"Heyyyy...youuu."

She looked at me, puzzled, as if a certain rat was controlling my movement and words under my ball cap.

"Uhhh...hi?" She passed me a funny look.

"H-h-how was class?"

"The class we were both just in?"

"Sure?"

"Okay, what's going on, Jason? Do you need help with your book report? If yes, there's no shame in asking from a superior mind."

"Ouch, thanks."

Just say the words!

"Listen, I..." My mind froze, causing a connection error to the words on my lips.

"...I'm listening?" She cocked her head to the side.

"I wanted to see if maybe, perhaps, should you be available, that..."

"I would like to go to the mythology exhibit this Friday with you?"

Took the words right out of my mouth. "I was gonna say Saturday."

"Uh-huh." She punched my arm.

I'll take a mind-reader for $400. "How did you know that I was gonna ask?"

She shrugged.

My point stands on the mind-reader. Man, I wish I had won that $400. "Fair enough."

A short yet lengthy silence stood between us. She blushed, *probably due to your choice of words, or lack thereof.*

"Sooo," I said. "Is that a yes?"

"How does 10:30 a.m. sound? You can pick me up then, and we'll head on over?"

"Yeah!" I said, as if I knew my schedule that far ahead. *You barely plan your breakfast out.* "10:30 works! Soooo...it's a date?"

"Yeah." She nodded, her tone turning serious. "It's a date."

* * *

As anyone can imagine, the first date is always the most nerve-wracking. I had to make sure I had all the essentials. *Phone? Check. Phone charger? Check. Wallet? Check. Full tank of gas? Check. Showered? Check. Tickets?...shoot...where are th...oh, check!*

The car ride there was a little awkward. When both are fully aware that it's a date, there is a tendency to perform. But after an awkward talk of "How was your morning?" we jumped into what we were excited to see.

"I cannot believe that there is an exhibit that has both King Tut and Pompeii artifacts." She clapped.

"Honestly. All this needs is the Dead Sea Scrolls, and it would be a masterpiece." I did a chef's kiss.

"Jason, they *do* have that."

I was flabbergasted. "Yo, what?"

"Yes! It's available to see. Well, some of it."

"Dang, that's insane...anything Roman-related?"

She scrolled through the website. "Mmmmm, doesn't look like it. But they do have a Byzantine section. Looks like it's on the...." She stared oddly at her phone.

"What?"

"...mythology of Jesus?"

"That's...one way to put it."

"Look, unless you're Tolkien or Lewis talking about Christianity being the 'true myth,' I take anyone calling Christianity a mythology with a grain of salt."

"Can't argue with that. But you also can't please them all."

Despite that little religious moment, we had a good talk on the drive. She had seen the Pompeii exhibit years ago at the California Science Center by USC. Her dad, being a history fanatic, took her to a lot of exhibits.

When we got to the Sarcophagus of King Tut (i.e., coffin), she was completely amazed. As if she were an archeologist herself, she was analyzing all positions of his resting place, and even more with the hieroglyphics. *The glass case certainly is not stopping her.*

"This is amazing. Over 3000 years later, we get to experience history." She beamed at me.

"You heard about the curse regarding his tomb?"

"The one about the financier of the excavation who died of a mosquito infection after opening the tomb?"

"I was referring to the other excavation archeologist who—"

"Died when his house caught on fire as he tried to retrieve his manuscript titled *The Egyptian Book of the Dead*?"

Dang, she's good.

"I know a lot of things, Jason. A lot of things." She gave a flirtatious smile.

Turns out she did. In each exhibit, she could lay out details that the average person would be oblivious to. Certain hieroglyphic meanings? She knew. Dead Ancient Nordic symbols? She understood. Certain gestures and meanings in Christian Holy Iconography? Without flaw. She was a walking textbook, one that drew you in both in its appearance and its insight.

What were a few hours felt like a whole day's worth of experiences as we spent every moment together in that museum. Afterward, while it was still warm out, we made our way to the museum garden, where we sat by the rose bushes for a picnic. Just the two of us were surrounded by some of the sweetest-smelling, most delicate variety of flowers we had ever seen.

"So, where do you store up all this history?" I scratched the back of my head. "Is this like a side hobby or a recent development?"

"My dad is former military, and with that came a lot of sites. Before meeting my mom, he would travel a lot, from

Germany to Rome, seeing things that only a handful of people probably will ever get the chance to see."

"Did y'all ever go together?"

"Unfortunately, no." She deflated at that. "When you bring kids into the mix, vacations like that are hard to come by."

"Yeah, it do be like that."

She giggled. "But that didn't stop my dad from trying to bring those places to us with exhibits like this." She paused. "Some of the earliest memories I have are at those museums with my parents. While my siblings would run off to anywhere else, I would stare at portraits and artifacts and read every book on the shelf, gathering every detail my mind could handle. I could never get enough of it."

How amazing is she? What a beautiful mind.

"That was one of the things I loved about my dad. From books to documentaries and exhibits, he always encouraged me to keep learning. The way he would tell stories growing up was like listening to a beloved book come to life. He was full of knowledge and passion in the stories he could recite.

She began to tear up. I was caught off guard. *Was my question too personal?*

"And then, one day, he passed."

"I'm so sorry, Gwen." I placed a hand on her shoulder. "I had no idea."

"It's okay. It's been a few years. Mom took it hard. While she has tried, it hasn't been easy on her, especially since I remind her so much of him." She took a moment to wipe her tears. "Before he passed, he asked us to promise him not to stop living and to find purpose, especially to her."

What a father she had. And a strong mother, too. I would give anything to see my dad have hope again.

She gathered her composure. "So, with that, I carry on my dad's legacy in continuing to learn and haven't stopped since."

"Wow," I say as if I could say anything else at that moment. "Your dad must've been extraordinary to talk with."

"Oh, you should have seen him at parties and events. Always talking away about his experiences."

I pondered this all.

As we continued our lunch, I began to share more about my background and the loss of my mother when I was thirteen. There was a sense of comfort in knowing we weren't alone in the loss of our parents. I informed her about how I fell into history when my mom showed me movies like *Gladiator* and *Braveheart*. She rolled her eyes when I mentioned *300*, the movie my mom steered clear of. I probably lost some brownie points on that one, but hey, it was truly a movie. While our parents were different in their own ways, they both emphasized the importance of storytelling and how it's important to live out our stories that will one day become part of history.

* * *

As we headed back to the school later that evening, we walked the long way back to her dorm.

"I had a great time with you today." She hid in her hoodie.

"I had a great time with you, too," I responded softly. "I appreciate you opening up about your family. That's not easy to go through."

"After years, I have been able to process things better. But yeah, he was something of a dad, and husband to my mom."

"I can see how much of an impact he had on you."

"Thanks. And thanks for bringing me; it was a lot of fun."

"Yeah, of course. I'm glad you got to enjoy it up close."

An awkward silence hovered between us.

"So, I'll hit you up again? Maybe for a second date?"

"Yeah. Maybe." She gave a tight smile. As we hugged

goodbye, I squeezed her shoulder. Maybe it was an extra second too long because my hand lingered there.

"Well, see you Sunday, Gwen." I walked off happily as if my body was warmed by her touch.

The following day, at the college fountain, while I was reading *The Four Loves* by C.S. Lewis, Gwen made her way over. We went in for a hug. "How was church?"

"It was good. Fr. Barron gave a great sermon on family in the church."

"Glad it went well. I don't want to keep you from where you're going, but I wanted to ask, any ideas on date number two?"

She looked at her shoes. "Jason, you are sweet."

Oh gosh, here it comes.

"And last night was great. I had such a great time with you."

"But?" I tried to hold it in.

"Last night gave me some perspective when I opened up about my dad and then heard you about your mom...I think I need to figure some things out before beginning a relationship."

"I see."

"And I don't mean that in a vague way." She took in a breath. "The loss of my dad took a toll I didn't expect. Loss is hard, as you know. When my dad had us promise to keep living, I meant that promise. And it's because of that, I think I need to put dating on hold, not just for school but to understand my vulnerabilities more when it comes to love and loss, starting with my mom. I can't change her, but I believe I need to work on my relationship with her before beginning a romantic one at this time."

I think you know she's right. While you were able to maintain a relationship with your dad after mom's passing, that came with time, too.

"I understand, Gwen." I sighed. "Losing people is a lot. I think you're doing the right thing."

She stared at me with a thankful smile and watery eyes.

"I'm not upset. I mean, I'm bummed out, but I'm not upset."

She gave a small laugh as if to laugh some pain away.

"I would rather you date when you feel ready to."

She enveloped me in a big hug. "Thank you." She sniffed some tears away as she pulled back.

"And hey," I said, "we'll always be friends. You can count on that."

She quickly nodded, not speaking.

Gwen was truly the one that got away, and to be honest, I was okay with that.

11
ANTI-FEMININE
NOAH

Hi, Noah,

You weren't answering your phone, so I figured email was the easiest way to contact you since it's going to be way too long to put into a text. I know it's been a long time since we've touched base on your play, but I'm afraid I have a bit of bad news.

You may remember our technical director—I believe you touched base with Simon during our drama camp. Well, he's being quite the stickler when it comes to this grant. I'm sure you remember his personality from drama camp and how he's very used to getting things his way.

He claims that he has a play, and (although I really shouldn't be saying this via the theater email for a variety of reasons) it's an absolute snooze-fest.

Unfortunately, seniority on the board often wins out. Although Simon is not our "President," for some reason, he acts like it. I think it has to do with the fact that he has his fingers wrapped around a lot of our sponsors. Theaters can't run on just dreams, you know.

The rest of the board and I agreed that we like your idea

much better, but until we can sway Simon to try to submit his play to a different contest, we're going to need to put a temporary hold on yours.

Sorry. I'll keep you posted. Let's hope that we can think of something else.

—Sarah

Noah frowned at the email as he scanned through it for a second time in his dorm. Leave it to his luck that the minute he'd asked a theater girl onto a platonic floor date that he'd miss the call from Sarah. The one that conveyed this information.

His mind veered back to the girl he'd requested to go on the group date with him. Like Gwen, she had no interest in pursuing anything in college—rendering her a safe pick.

As his eyes flicked back to the email, his thoughts raced.

Now what? So many guys and girls hinged their hopes on him, that he would voice their woes, their hurts...so some part of their past could graduate. And leave them alone to heal.

If it never made it to the stage, all their words would die with him.

An idea sprung into his head as the sound of a whoosh came from the bathroom. He'd seen a few freshmen chucking various bath-related objects down the toilet. If he needed to go, he'd have to seek refuge in another floor's restroom.

Flipping open the lid to his computer, he rattled a quick message to their college theater director.

Hi, Professor Reed!

I know I've already done my directing class, but I was wondering if I could swing something by you. I've written a play (well, mostly written a play) and am wondering if I could steal the black box as a performance space. So we can workshop this play and do a performance.

Minimal props, minimal sets, and any additional expenses will be on me.

I've attached what I have, but I'd love to bring this to the stage. Let me know what this looks like.

—Noah

For the next hour, he picked away at a tedious paper for one of his remaining gen eds. *Should've knocked those out my freshman and sophomore years.* In his defense, with his loaded theater schedule, he couldn't accommodate more than 16 credits per semester without his brain exploding.

To his surprise, ninety minutes after he'd queried Professor Reed, another email popped up in his inbox. A short one.

Hey, Noah,

I'm in my office right now. Why don't we plan to talk about it here?

—Professor Reed

His heart skipped so much that he felt his intestines liquify. Fighting the urge to re-read the email for more clues as to whether a) she read it, b) hated it, or c) saw promise in it, he threw his messenger bag over one shoulder and charged out into the wintry bitterness on campus.

Regret roiled his gut, the only heat source against the chilly wind, as he realized he should've proofed the play. Should've added a few more scenes.

His schedule had consumed so much of his time that he'd watched weeks flit past without adding much to the script.

Oh well, can't do anything about it now.

Heaters singed his cold ears when he stepped into the

theater building. A fellow thespian, who had a shock of red hair, typed away on a laptop. He was stationed in one of the chairs by the staircase that led up to the auditorium.

They locked eyes, and the redhead gaped. "Noah?"

"Erm." Noah searched his memory recesses for the name of the student who often landed Ensemble and one-line roles. "Weston?"

"Yeah!" Weston's roan eyes alighted, perhaps an indication that he was happy to be remembered, even if in name. "You're the guy writing that play, right? Any chance I could pick your brain?"

Noah glanced over his shoulder at a large clock that hung from the ceiling.

"Eh, I'm already running late for something." He had no idea how long Professor Reed's office hours lasted, but he didn't want to risk it. "Any chance we could raincheck?"

Weston deflated, but Noah watched the fabricated smile stretch across his face. "Yeah, no problem." Huh, maybe Professor Reed should've given Weston some better roles; he could play the part of an actor well.

Noah sailed past him and darted to Professor Reed's office. The door had already cracked open, but he knocked against it anyway.

"Enter."

He did so and sank into a plush, worn red chair. Professor Reed typed the finishing touches on what looked to be an email from his vantage point. Then she smoothed out her purple scarf and turned to him.

"I had no idea you were a writer." She blinked at him over glittery spectacles.

"I mean." He palmed his neck. "I had a lot of help editing it with a professional writing student, but yeah. Thought we'd give it a go."

Left out the part about getting rejected by Sarah's theater.

That would probably lessen the professor's opinion of the play.

"Well, I'm impressed. We've had a few playwrights in our program, but mostly, we teach students trying to go the directing or acting route."

A shockwave was sent through his system.

She liked it?

Hope catapulted into his throat and threatened to choke him with tremors.

"So...about the black box space—"

Professor Reed held up a hand as bracelets clinked down her wrists. She unsheathed her glasses and clipped them onto her breast pocket.

"I think you are incredibly talented in many ways, Noah. One of my star students in the program."

He anticipated the but.

"We..." She sighed. "I noticed in the play that a lot of the perspectives are from males. I know you had a few female monologues in there, but it's clear that it's airing out the grievances of guys. I'm not entirely sure how our audience—who typically veers more female—will handle that."

Knots formed in his insides. He gripped the chair and felt his knuckles whiten.

"I mean, we could gender-swap a few roles." He recalled Sarah's suggestion. "But I think the point of the play is that we all seem to have a hard time navigating dating at college."

"True." She clicked her tongue, perhaps unaware of her involuntary tic. "And I know, being a conservative Christian college, we're far from being feminist warriors. Well." She smirked. "Most of us, anyway."

Ah, he recalled she'd put on several of what would've been called "progressive" plays by Mansfield standards. His mind rushed through the scenes of his script, and worry furrowed his brow. Did he come off too harsh to females? Not presenting their perspective fairly enough? He had used their exact words and didn't know what else he could add or do.

"I mean, maybe I could do some clean-up."

The professor shook her head. "I'm afraid it goes beyond that. If people see that a male wrote a play on dating—and that many moments seem decidedly anti-female, we're going to get a lot of backlash. In the campus paper, in the community..."

He bristled at this.

Did he write something that anti-feminine? Sarah had never voiced so.

Maybe the professor's seeing something we're not. "I'm sorry. It's not my intention to be offensive."

"You didn't offend me." Her voice had softened. "And your play isn't any of those things. I'm just anticipating the kind of feedback we'd get on this sort of thing. PR and theater are a delicate balance."

A storm of emotions tugged him in each direction of the office. Toward the playbills with cast signatures, in the direction of the professor's SAG-AFTRA membership papers.

"What I don't understand..." He clasped his hands. "If this play was all from the female perspective, we'd put it on, right? No hesitation?"

She tilted her hand back and forth. "Probably would get some conservatives on campus upset, but yes, that would be seen as innovative."

"So why is it that when guys go through something hard, we're not allowed to voice that? We just have to grin and bear it because 'we're the cause of all problems.'"

She met him with a pitying expression. "It's a beautiful play, Noah. One I'm sure a theater will be happy to put on. Just not here."

"I understand." He stood and looped his bag over his shoulder. "Thanks for your time."

As he headed back to the double doors that led outside, Weston stood. Then sat back down. His mouth dropped, words brimming on the tip of his tongue, unspoken.

"Still need to pick my brain?" Noah doubled back, unsure if he should inform Weston about the most recent development.

"Yeah." Weston wrung his hands. "If you're not busy."

12
INDECISIVE MUCH?
WESTON

Abigail was something. I knew her for some time before college. We attended the same church and the same high school. Everyone knew who she was, given her involvement. Choir? Check. Theater? Check. Orchestra? Check. If something existed in performing arts, she did it. Also, randomly, she had a big love for horses.

Not only was she gifted, but she seemed to get any guy she wanted. She dated the captain of every major school sports team and was Prom Queen twice, where she dated the Prom Kings afterward. *Those guys are the luckiest in Indiana.*

As for me, I was a friend in her eyes. We attended the same classes and were in choir together. Heck, we even had a duet in our showcase choir performance that got us first place in the state. I honestly liked her a lot but hardly found the courage to make a move. That all changed when we hit college.

She and I were in the same ministry organization, one that worked with Christian clubs at public high schools. We were partners for two schools and spent a lot of time together. In that, we grew closer.

"You honestly have liked me since high school?"

"Well," I blushed, "yeah. I mean, you were just fun to be around and had a heart for the arts and ministry, and I admire that about you."*Dang, you're getting really honest with her.*

"Weston, that's sweet."

My face turned a deeper shade of red. *She's taking this a lot better than expected.*

"Can I tell you something?" She tilted her head to the side.

"Uh, sure." My heart pounded my chest even more.

"You...never mind, it's embarrassing." She turned her reddened face from me.

I leaned forward. "No, say what you want to."

She took in a deep breath, letting a beat pass to gather her words. "Okay. As you might know, I dated a lot in high school."

"What? Really?" I playfully muttered. She giggled as she lightly punched my arm.

"Meanie. But yeah, I dated a lot of guys, and they didn't last long. To keep it short, they weren't exactly kind."

"Oh?"

"I felt as if they weren't dating me for me. As if they were dating me for my status."

I frowned. "I'm sorry you went through that."

"Which is why, with you, I feel different. You have always been genuine and kind. I see the loyalty you have to loved ones in your life, and that is just...something you don't see often."

Our first few dates were wonderful. We visited a couple of state fairs, watched a lot of bad movies, and had "homework" dates. At first, these were fun. As time went on, it felt as if we were *just* having fun. So, I figured we'd ease into our next steps.

"You want to meet my parents?" Her eyebrows drew apart, her expression reading either confused or surprised.

"Well, yeah. Granted, I met them in high school, but I figured they would want to know who you're dating and all."

"Weston, I appreciate you being forward, but don't you think it's a bit too fast?" She bit her bottom lip.

"Oh." *Too fast? It's been three months. And that's with us being good childhood friends.* "Do you feel that's too fast? I'm sorry if so. I just assumed three months was a good amount of time."

"Well yeah, it's been a few weeks or so, but we haven't even defined the relationship."

"Oh. I'm sorry. It kinda felt like we did through our dates."

"I think it would be best if we had a formal talk about it." She held my hands, calming my panicked look. "You know, to get to know intentions and life goals more."

Despite being puzzled, I had an idea of what she meant. "Okay. Shall we define it now?" *Dude! She just said don't rush it!*

"In time, Wes. In time." She gave me a soft kiss on the cheek. "I have a group project meeting to get through. See you later tonight?"

"Yeah, sure." I turned red. *I hope she doesn't think I was pushy. I don't want to be one of those Nice-Guy types.*

I tried to understand where she was coming from. Given her dating history, I figured she needed time. That said, close friends were confused by her approach.

"I'm just saying, bro," my roommate Taylor commented, "it sounds like she's stringing you along."

"Abi isn't like that." I exhaled a sharp breath.

"Don't you think it's kinda weird that it's been nearly four months, and you still haven't had a DTR?"

"She just needs time."

"And over three months isn't enough?"

"Look, I gotta get to class." *If 'going to class' thirty minutes early means avoiding this conversation, then so be it.* "We'll talk later."

"I don't think I'm the one you need to talk to. Weston, you're a great friend and have been loyal and caring. Don't you think you deserve that from Abi?"

I pondered his words. "Fine, I'll try and talk to her about it on our date later tonight. Happy?"

Taylor was looking out for me. He was my first friend in college since we both found out we graduated from rival high schools. We bonded over music and movies and grew closer at our church. I didn't see why he'd steer me wrong, but *he just doesn't understand the situation.*

Later that day, Abigail and I headed to the mall to go shopping. As we went through the clearance section at Old Navy, I began to feel uneasy. The thought of what Taylor said lingered as it played over and over. *You have to say something. You have given a lot in four months. Maybe she's ready for all you know.*

We sat in the food court after ordering Chinese. She talked about something choir-related, but my mind kept getting distracted. *Do I say it or not? Do I say it or not?*

"Weston!" She scrunched her brows at me.

I suddenly returned to reality, almost forgetting where I was.

"What's gotten into you today? You hardly said a word back at Old Navy and completely zoned out over dinner."

"I'm sorry. I just, uhh..." I scrambled to gather my thoughts.

"Just...what? Is everything okay?"

It's now or never, bro. "Abi." I cleared my throat. "Abi. I have been doing some thinking."

"I could tell, given how long you blanked out for." She giggled.

"I think we should define our relationship."

Her smile faded. "Right now?"

"Yeah. I mean, we can right now, if that's okay. I was speaking in general."

She moved her elbows off the table, away from me. Then she folded her arms, scoffing. "You're doing this right now?"

"I…it's been four months. I get that I may have come off strong back then about your parents—"

"Which you did." She raised her eyebrows.

I stumbled in my words as if my breath was pulled out of my lungs. "I…I really care about you. I want to pursue you." She scrunched into herself, a sign of being uncomfortable. "And I hope that you feel the same for me, hence the DTR."

She gathered her thoughts for a few seconds, mumbling something under her breath. "You think I'm not pursuing you? Is that it?"

"No, that's not what I meant. I meant that I just want us to be on the same—"

"Is me going out with you and giving you the time of day not enough for you?"

I stopped. *Is she…no, she can't be.*

"Okay. Love, I was only—"

"Please, don't call me that." She tossed up a hand.

My fingers began to get clammy as my mind refused to slow down. *Okay, dude, control yourself. Just keep it cool.* "Abi. I just think that maybe we should at least talk about what we want, for the two of us, in this relationship."

"Well, what I want is to go home."

I was dumbfounded. *Didn't she like my honesty? Isn't that what you're supposed to do in relationships?*

"Okay." I breathed in heavily, hand pressed to my mouth as I gathered my thoughts. "Abi, I'm not trying to make you uncomfortable. I am never trying to make you feel questioned or cornered. It's just…you're really important to me. And I want us to trust each other as a couple."

The awkward silence rang for an eternity. She hardly made eye contact with me. She checked her phone for a second and then put it back into her pocket.

"Take me home."

If a few silent seconds felt like an eternity, the car ride back to her dorm felt like purgatory. When we parked at her dorm, she shot out of the car. No goodbye. Just a slammed door. At that moment, time stood still. *Taylor is right. I'm saying something.*

"Abi." I darted toward her.

"I said I want to be left alone." She kept walking without turning around.

"Did you do this with all the guys you dated?" I shot back. "Or is there something about me that doesn't add up?"

She stopped in her tracks and turned, appearing irritated. "What do you mean by that?"

"You know what I mean. Ever since we first talked about going out, it has been nothing but fun and games. And that's fine, honestly. I love hanging out with you. But this, our relationship, is something beyond that. But every time I bring it up, you change the subject, get angry with me, or suddenly have a group project meeting you forgot about." A silence sliced between us. She hardly stared at me as she kept her arms folded. "Do you even want to date me?"

"Of course I do, Weston. It's just—"

"Just what? Am I doing something wrong? Because I don't understand how wanting to move forward is."

"I want to keep my options open."

This halted me. *She's...she's dating other guys?* "You. You what?"

"I don't think I'm ready for any long-term commitment, and I don't want to miss out on better options.

Better options?? "So while you're seeing other guys, I'm just your boy toy that you play with whenever the others don't work out?"

"Weston, it's not like that. Please listen—"

"No. You listen to me. If you want to date other guys that you think are better for you, then fine. Do what you want. But I am not going to be one of your guys that's stuck in a game of Russian roulette." I walked back to my car and drove off. They say you shouldn't cry over rejection. That day, I didn't care.

13
EMOTIONAL STAKES
NOAH

"And you're sure you're okay?" Noah asked.

Em peered at Noah through the FaceTime call with droopy lips, eyebrows raised. Right. She was proposed to by her cheating boyfriend, with her parents taking *his* side...no one could bounce back from that in a matter of days.

"I meant, did you manage to get to your friend's house okay? Since you're staying away from your parents for the rest of winter break."

Em lifted herself from a beanbag and gave him the grand tour. A Christmas tree, still up from the holiday a few days ago, twinkled with fairy lights. Stockings hung from a fake fireplace, with two other socks strung up haphazardly. Harmony and Em stayed with a friend over winter break, so the family must've put those up to make them feel included.

Then, Em showed her jagged painted nails to the camera.

"The two of them are out, picking up some Chinese food, but we did some manicures before that. Anything to paint over my Mom's bait-and-switch."

He frowned in the coffee shop, turning his ear to the

phone. A bean grinder had mixed up those words in his brain. "Huh?"

"Oh, maybe I didn't tell you—Mom took me out for manicures as an 'apology' for her and Dad fighting over Christmas. I thought it was an olive branch, but apparently, it was just for the proposal. She wanted my nails to look nice for the pictures. It was so embarrassing when they had to explain to the photographer that I said no."

Pride swelled in Noah for Em turning down her now-ex, Frankie.

He'd never liked that guy. Some poor excuse for a man who gave Em slobbery kisses as a Christmas gift, even when she recoiled. He'd dominated Em's schedule, and the minute Em decided to do practices for the annual school lip sync battle, he went behind her back to talk with his old ex.

"Well, I'm glad you painted over your nails. It's, erm, very artistic."

"Yeah, Harmony says my nails are skinny and make a difficult canvas, but it's fine. I can always remove the paint later." She returned to her beanbag, and the red fabric filled the background of the screen. "Anyway, how are you faring?"

Did she want to know?

Or have the capacity to know?

So many of their conversations had turned strained this year. If only Em could give up that stupid bet so she...

What? Can you spend more time with me? Now I sound like some clingy boyfriend.

He just wanted to see the life spark into her eyes again since they appeared to dim every moment now. And if he could be the one to do it...

He eyed his laptop with the draft of his GoFundMe.

I'm pulling the trigger on that today. Hopefully, in the next five months, he could collect enough for the $20k. A little difficult, though, if he couldn't share on social media. She followed all his accounts.

"I'm..." He sipped his chai and frowned at how it had turned lukewarm. How much time had he spent on the call? "Fine."

Em's eyes narrowed. Not buying it.

"Anything going on in my life is paling compared to yours." He hadn't even told her the update about the school refusing to put on his play. And the local theater bowing out due to Simon.

For all Em knew, he'd take some of the stories she'd shared with him and put them on a stage—kickstarting his playwriting career.

But it felt silly to burden her with that now.

Em's hair butterflied behind her, and Noah, for some odd reason, felt like she'd be an absolute vision with flowers placed on it, like some Ophelia in a pond in a painting.

For some reason, he didn't shake the thoughts away this time. Instead, he kept them like a late Christmas gift to himself.

"Mkay, I won't push you, Noah, but I hope you realize it's important for guys to express their emotions and feelings, too."

He snorted. Then, he stopped when he met her cold stare.

"Sorry, it's just...people say that all the time, but they never really mean it." He halted. "I mean, obviously not you. You're a very honest person, but—"

Her eyes narrowed to the point where he couldn't even see the pupils in the squint. "But what?"

"People say stuff all the time like, 'guys should be able to ask for help' and 'Jesus wept too,' but the minute one of us does, people tell us we're too much. That we're supposed to be the strong ones and keep it together."

Em's features softened.

For the first time in months, pity laced into her expression. Maybe she'd experienced a gut punch of humility from the proposal.

"About what I'd said about men being trash..." She rolled her eyes. "I mean, Frankie *is* trash. But I think I'm starting to see why you're writing that play."

Saliva caught in his dry throat. "Yeah?"

"Yeah. Someone has to be a voice for people who are hurting like that. I mean..." She blinked away a glaze as her eyes rimmed red. They'd been puffy on nearly every call he'd fielded. "I can't imagine what a mess I'd be if Harmony's friend didn't let me stay with her. If you'd been in my situation, would you have gone for help?"

He choked down the lump in his throat.

No, he wouldn't have.

If his parents were anything like Em's—which, thank goodness, their "meanness" ended with their disapproval of his career choices and some of their dubious business practices—he would've endured the toxic home environment. Until he wilted into a snakeskin of himself, a former shadow of Noah.

"Keep writing that thing, Noah." She winked at the camera. "I have a feeling it could do a lot of good." The sound of a door slamming punctured the phone. "Ah, looks like they're home. Gotta go."

After Noah had signed off, he blew out a long breath.

Why keep writing if it would never reach the stage? Sarah hadn't sent any updates, and all the theaters within a thirty-mile radius of Mansfield either ghosted him or said they didn't take unpublished plays. Speaking of publishing, when he turned to play publishers online, they said they wouldn't put on a play if it had never been performed before.

So you can't win. No wonder most people didn't make a career out of playwriting.

He'd cast the bait for one last chance, a local theater director in his hometown who had attended Mansfield ten years ago. Noah had joined the school for that very reason. In high school, he'd enjoyed working with this director and wanted to end up just like him.

The shop bell dinged as the door opened, and a husk of Director Jeremy entered. Bags pulled at his eyes, and he hunched into his peacoat. The red that rimmed Em's eyes echoed in his waterline.

He trudged up to the register, placed his order, and sat.

"Hey, man." Noah winced. "If this isn't a good day..."

Director Jeremy tossed up a hand and went to retrieve his drink. Coffee, black, no frills. Noah didn't recall correctly, but he could've sworn Jeremy read as more of a latte kind of guy. Maybe life had changed in the four years he'd gone off to college.

"To be honest with you, Noah." He sipped the bitter brew, grimaced, and cinched his eyes shut as if he'd just received a knockout punch to the abdomen. "There's not going to be a 'good' day to approach this. Not this week."

Noah steeled himself for the why.

In the last five months, he'd subjected himself to difficult dating tales. And with Em's recent proposal, he didn't know how much more bad news he could handle.

"I'm sorry, man."

Jeremy sighed. "It's honestly worse than you think."

Did a close relative die? Noah had perused Jeremy's social media before this meeting for any hints of life updates, anything he could latch onto for a pitch for his play, or at least, a conversation starter.

But that elevator speech for his play faded into the background.

Jeremy looked less lively than a corpse, and it wouldn't be fair to bring up the show.

Noah sighed. He recalled what Em had said on the call. If he didn't create an outlet for Jeremy, no one else would.

"Try me."

Jeremy's eyes traced the gouges taken out of their high-top table. "My wife served me divorce papers. On Christmas."

A chill settled over his bones.

In high school, he'd recalled their proposal. Jeremy and his then-girlfriend had co-directed *Phantom* together. During their final dress rehearsal, during "All I Ask of You," the actor playing Raoul handed Jeremy a red rose. To which, he bent on one knee and asked the woman sitting in the front row to marry him.

The entire theater had whooped and hollered. And the trumpet players in the pit blarped (blared and burped) a gleeful note for the occasion.

They'd called them the ultimate couple.

The perfect pairing.

And now?

An icy chuckle escaped Jeremy's lips. "Told you it was bad."

"I'm...wow." Noah slumped back against his seat, feeling it teeter. He balanced himself. "That's awful."

"It is...so as you can imagine, even if our theater *could* put on a play about relationships that you sent me...I'm not sure if I'd have the heart to do something like that after this."

The deflation lasted just a moment. Noah shook it off. Jeremy had witnessed the murder of a beautiful marriage. That took precedence now.

"Don't worry about it, man. It's probably a good thing that it's not getting picked up by any place, anyway. If it would cause that much damage."

Jeremy blinked. "Damage?"

"Yeah, you just said you wouldn't be able to put it on, given what—" He searched for the right words. There were none, not for this. "Happened to you. Maybe I'd ruin the lives of a bunch of people if it were ever brought to the stage."

Words from his professor haunted him about how the play would incite the ire of ladies across campus and the community.

Maybe he should never pick up a pen again.

"Whoa, whoa." For the first time that day, a spark filled Jeremy's cheeks with color. "I just said that I couldn't direct it *personally*. Engaging with that material daily within the first few weeks of something like what I went through." He clutched his chest. "The wounds are too fresh to be involved in that way. But, dude." He aimed a weak punch at Noah's shoulder. "It's a really good play."

Noah hated himself for how much glee filled him at that moment. That somber moment where he should've shared in the grief of a friend.

But he couldn't help it. Someone thought he had talent.

"Really?"

"Yeah, I hope someone does this. I'm not sure if anyone in my contacts is open to unpublished plays, but I could poke around. See if I can chase any leads for you."

Noah penciled that idea in for later.

"Sure, but don't worry about this meeting today for a long time, dude. You're going through a lot."

Jeremy smirked, nodded, and chucked his cup into a bin behind him. As he rose, he froze and turned back.

"Question: Is it just the story of Mansfield students who are currently attending?"

"Erm...I think that's been the majority, but we've had a few professors contribute if that's what you're asking." Many of the female professors had offered monologue material, and one male professor reached out. And Sarah. She had promised to send her story before the whole Simon incident went down at the theater.

An internal battle waged across Jeremy's face. He opened his mouth, drew in a sharp breath...

"Any chance you'd be willing to talk with an alum? Even if it doesn't end up being performed, it may be helpful to get the words out."

Noah's lips quirked into a grin. "I'm sure we can find room in the schedule."

14
ONLY GOOD MEMORIES
JEREMY

Millie and I first met the weekend we graduated. She got a B.A. in Art; I earned mine in Communications Management. It's funny how you can have multiple classes together and still not know someone until years later. We met at a mutual friend's graduation party and hit it right off right away.

She sat opposite me in a group, and I noticed her after she asked me about my internship. We got talking right away about common interests. Books, Marvel movies, art, history, the list goes on. As everyone was partying and celebrating, we just talked on the couch as if time itself stood still at that moment. She was truly a remarkable woman.

As you can imagine, we started dating a few weeks later, and in that short time, we came to learn much about each other.

"Millie, your work is amazing."

"You think so?" Dimples formed in her cheeks.

"Yes! You have so much potential. I've never seen anything like it."

"That...that means a lot." She paused. "My last boyfriend didn't invest much into my dreams or interests."

"I am so sorry that happened." My heart felt heavy for her. "How could someone do that? Relationships are a team effort."

"Yeah, you would think so. He was one-dimensional. Only good times were important to him."

"How do you mean?" I never heard anyone say it like that.

"So, you know how relationships require growth?"

"Of course."

"And growth involves hard times, conflict, and change."

"Mmmhmm."

She sighed and let out a rueful laugh.

"He didn't want that. No growth. No depth. The minute something bad came along." She snapped her fingers. "Gone."

"That's ridiculous."

"As you can imagine, it came to an end. And while I was the one to end it, he got what he wanted in the end."

I remained silent. "How awful. I am so sorry."

"Thanks." She passed me a soft smile.

A pause enveloped us.

"Hey," I said. She looked up, embarrassed. "I would never do that to you. Your dreams are important. And if they're important to you, they're important to me."

She blushed in her smile, causing a tear to form but never fall.

We ended the day visiting a museum at the last minute that varied from Greco-Roman architecture to Renaissance art. Among all the art in the room that displayed beauty, she was the most beautiful depiction in the room. Cheesy, I know. Any of my theater students would've groaned at that. But let's be honest. They would've eaten it up, too.

So much of theater is about love. About understanding

the human emotions that are so hard to put into words. So we act them out instead.

We talked for hours about our love for history, and as our conversation came to an end, our lips touched for the first time. Nothing in that moment mattered. All I could think and feel was her.

In the year that followed, the honeymoon phase was enjoyable and full of unforgettable memories, but it didn't come without its challenges. Student loans kicked in, and the economy was struggling. While our personal lives were affected, our work lives did so as well.

I was early in my public relations career and moved up pretty quickly. I went from intern to administrative assistant early on. After years of retail work and "school credit" summer gigs, I was finally getting somewhere. While that was going on, she was struggling to enter her career.

"Is everything all right, love?"

"It's nothing." She swiped a small tear away.

Despite her performance here, I knew she wasn't one to necessarily hold back tears. She embraced emotions like a barefoot person embraced the rain and puddles for splashing.

And as always, I'd embrace that storm with her. "Love, you know I can tell when something is bothering you. I don't want to push you if you aren't ready to say it. Just know that I am here."

She took a deep breath. "Love, I am happy for you moving up in your career, and you know you have my support." She paused. "I am just worried that I won't be enough for you."

"Millie, of course I don't think less of you. You are more than enough. Where is this coming from?" I gripped her hands.

"It's just." She teared up. "I don't want you to think I'm a burden. That I am incapable of landing on my feet or that we drift apart as a result."

"Is this because of *La La Land* movie night last week?"

She giggled as she cleaned her tears away. "A little. I just don't want us to become like them is all."

"Hey, it's a movie. And we are not like them. We put each other first and encourage each other's ambitions. You're gonna make it. You're gonna land on your feet, and when you do, I will be right there, cheering you on and supporting you. Okay?"

"And I for you."

Roughly a year later, I was looking to propose. Her parents were beyond supportive of us, along with mine. We got married a short amount of time after that. It was the best day of my life. And while that was going on, my career was growing to where I was made Public Relations Director at the firm. Meanwhile, she was promoted to Assistant Manager in retail. That first year was truly something.

But in the year that followed, changes for the worse would come, slowly but surely. Through my old church, I overheard a friend of a friend who needed artists for hire. To keep it short, she owned an art gallery that was looking to expand for new artists to enter the industry. Millie was nervous at first, given how much she endured just to even get a foot in the door.

"I don't think I can do this."

"Love," I responded, "this has your name written all over it. It's perfect for you."

Her eyes reflected the light as tears began to form. "I just...I think it will kill me if I do."

"What?"

"Love, I appreciate this, but I don't think I can take another no."

I clasped her hands. "Babe. You have to do this."

"Why? I have been rejected by countless galleries and submissions. How will this possibly be any different?"

"Because I know you. I've seen your work. You have everything to make it work." I kissed her forehead.

"You're only saying that because you're my husband."

Still, her shove was playful.

"And it's because I'm your husband that I know you deep down as much as you know me." I pressed my forehead to hers.

Her expression morphed from playful to scared. I heard her breath getting shallow.

"Honey, breathe. You're okay."

"I-I-I."

"I know."

Her palms buried her emotional expressions. I gently pulled back her hands, seeing her most vulnerable. "I know you have everything in you to do this."

"I don't think I can stand up and fight for myself again."

"Then I will stand and fight for you."

After some time, she agreed to contact the Art Director. Lo and behold, one connection led to another. She impressed her at that first meeting and more in that first gallery. Next thing you know, Millie not only had more art displayed, but also got offered to be Assistant Director. She always had an act of wowing people.

We both loved theater in high school, and by now, I was helping at a local theater, so we both lived for a performance. I directed people to perform on the stage. She was much better at carrying her acting skills with her off of the stage.

As is always the case with good times, you can only suffer those so much before the bad ones surface. And yes, I do mean suffer. Good times wrap you up in so much ignorance and bliss that you get sidelined when the bad seasons loom.

Despite the promotion I received, the year was rough,

resulting in bad fiscal numbers and a scandal with one of our clients, a fire that took months to put out. As a result, layoffs began, with me included.

When she was struggling in her career, I did what I could to help her with encouragement and reassurance. But when the roles were reversed, she didn't.

While I was able to freelance for various clients, Millie was not having it.

"I don't understand how you haven't been able to find work."

"I mean, love, I've been putting out roughly fifty job apps a week on top of completing freelance work. The economy isn't exactly great right now."

"I understand, babe, but I've been the main income for a while now, and frankly, it's been tiresome."

"Tiresome? You're on a fixed income."

"Yes, but it still falls on me to keep everything up. One wrong move, and maybe they'll demote or fire me."

"I am trying to do everything I can. It's just hard right now."

Her jaw dropped. "You're doing everything you can?"

"Yes, I am."

She took a deep breath. "Honestly, babe, I don't think you are."

I was completely stunned. "I'm sorry?"

Ringing filled my ears for a moment.

"I don't think you're trying as hard because if you were, if you were putting yourself out there as you say, then you would have landed something by now. Meanwhile, I moved up in my job. I have been able to push myself into my career."

"Okay, that's not exactly a fair comparison. I got you that connection."

She rolled her eyes. She *hated it* when I pointed this out.

"Yeah, and then I did the rest of the work to get me where I am."

The room went silent.

Like an audience after a character gave a zinger of a line.

But all theater nerds know an audience hates dead air. Millie knew this, too, and plowed forward.

"Love, you keep applying for jobs in your field as if you could get your spot back...don't you think maybe you need to downgrade to something more suitable for your expertise?"

That felt like a gut punch. Sure, on her salary, our budget was tight. But we could make it a little longer, hold out a little longer. Were we in more dire circumstances, I would try for something in retail or food service. But as it already was, I'd applied for jobs that were major pay cuts.

"You did not just say that right now."

"Well, your plan isn't working. Maybe it's time to..."

"To what? To give up on what I worked hard for?"

"Well, maybe you need to take a crappy job before you get back to having a real job."

Millie loved dramatic exits and took one after that conversation to drive around the neighborhood to "cool off." We didn't address that conversation again and pretended it hadn't happened.

Life after was dividing. Our dates felt more like obligations, and dinners were more lonely with two people in the room. I eventually took a lower-paying position. Nothing remotely related to public relations. Just an Executive Assistant. I thought that since I got a job now, maybe she would be relieved and happy, that we would mend what we broke. But as time went on, she grew in her job as Art Director. She was busier now than ever, attending galleries and building connections over second-rate wine and cheese events...without me.

It wasn't that I was too busy; she didn't invite me. At one

point, I mentioned visiting to support her, but she immediately shot it down. The spark in our marriage was giving out. I never felt more alone in a shared home.

Every time I would mention marriage counseling or having a talk with our priest, Millie wouldn't have it. I couldn't understand why she didn't want to fix our marriage... until I came home to her...and a lawyer.

"What's...going on?"

"I should give you two some space." The lawyer awkwardly walked out the door, passing by me with a forced half-smile. I'd always assumed lawyers met people in offices, but maybe some did home visits.

And besides, what was more important was *why the heck was he just here?*

"Honey, who was that?"

"Jeremy." She patted the couch, her voice cold. Scarily calm. That wasn't like Millie. "Please, sit."

In that motion to sit, it felt as if time had slowly passed. My stomach churned as my legs began to shake. At that moment, all I could hear was the increasing rate of my heart as it awaited the shattering news.

"There is no easy way to say this...I want a divorce."

So this is it. The day I tried to prevent was inevitable.

"Honey." Tears blinded my eyes. "Tell me."

"Jeremy, we have been growing apart for some time now. You know we have."

"Th-th-that's why." I struggled to make sense of my words and my thoughts. "I wanted us t-t-go into counseling."

"Honey, it was over long before that."

I took a deep breath, trying to hold everything back. "Baby...what did I do wrong?"

"Jeremy."

"I left my career. I got a new job. I did everything I could to make you feel secure, provided, and cared for. I know we haven't had it easy in our fights lately, but I have never once thought about leaving you."

"But I have."

There it was. Another zinger line. I could just picture the theater audience recoiling from the impact of those words.

It took everything in me not to fall on my knees, begging for her to stay. I kept everything in as much as possible as if showing my emotional strength would change her mind. But then she said it.

"Jeremy, we have made many memories together in our marriage and before, memories I wouldn't trade for the world."

But you were willing to trade me away for the world?

"But if you take away those good memories, there's not much left."

As if my soul left my body, I had no control over my movements.

"John, the lawyer," she slowly said, showing little emotion. "He'll need the paper filed next week. You technically have thirty days, but I don't think this is something to drag your feet about, do you?" She got up to leave for another art exhibit. Millie could be dramatic on her own time, but not when she had a schedule to keep.

As she went for the exit, I couldn't bring myself to look in her direction.

"Know that I loved you and wanted anything but this to happen for us."

She walked out, slowly closing the door behind her.

There I was, alone in my home. My prison.

Never before had I let out a cry so deep, so painful toward God, toward anyone who would listen. I wept uncontrollably on that couch. All the hope that I had left in our marriage slowly drained out like a river of blood bleeding out of a corpse that knew not what nor why it deserved what came its way.

Will I ever find joy in love again? Will it ever get better? Will this pain remain forever? Nothing but questions remained in my mind as I did nothing but weep and blame myself for not fighting harder. But how can one expect to fight harder for someone who doesn't want to be fought for to begin with?

15

UNHEARD

NOAH

"Is Em here?" Noah asked.

Harmony, clad in a Frosty the Snowman onesie, deflated when Noah entered their apartment and asked this question. Often, the four ladies who lived here left the door unlocked until after hours in the evening.

She bit her bottom lip, leaped up from the futon, and raced over to the oven in time to pull out some slightly burnt sweet potato fries. She waved a cool pan over the hot one.

"She's probably out crying or something." Harmony rolled her eyes.

Noah had no idea what had gone down between winter break and the months leading up until now, but he knew Harmony and Em weren't talking. Perhaps Harmony had carried too many of Em's emotional burdens after the proposal. *Who knows?*

When Harmony had deemed the fries cool enough, she sheathed her hands in oven mitts and dumped the contents into a bowl. Scooping up a bowl of some kind of dip, she brought both over to the couch and patted the seat next to her.

"Hungry?" She batted her eyelashes at him.

Ah, here we go again.

Harmony had gotten it in her head that she had a crush on him and thought she was being incredibly sneaky, except for the fact that Harmony's flirting styles included laughing loud enough to shake the walls and punching the arm of the said object of her affection.

He'd watched it go down at the hoedown with Harmony's former ex, and Noah's arm had retained a few bruises from recent encounters.

Shielding his shoulder with his hand, he parked in a chair adjacent to the couch. Once again, Harmony flattened from disappointment. Any less air in her, and she'd sit like a broken balloon against the couch.

Still, she grabbed a side table, moved it in front of him, and set the contents down.

"Eat."

And he did so. Because even if he rejected Harmony's advances, and even in a snowman onesie, the girl could be intimidating. He swirled the fries in a green sauce and prayed Harmony's cooking didn't match her eclectic style.

As he crunched on the crispy fries, he mmm'd. "Is that wasabi?"

"Horseradish. There's a burger place back home that makes really good sweet potato fries and a dip to go with it." The light had returned to her eyes, and she bounced up and down on the couch.

"Are you sure you want me eating all of these?" He'd already chowed down on five in the time it took Harmony to get out her sentence. "I'm sure you were going to eat them."

"Nah. I figured I needed to do something with my hands. These lip sync battle practices have got me all frantic."

He'd heard stories of practices for the school tradition going until midnight. Too bad his theater schedule wouldn't allow him to participate. He imagined that if he grouped a bunch of thespians, and they sang from *Hamilton*, they could claim first prize.

"Well." He lifted a fry in a salute. "Thanks for feeding me. I think I forgot about lunch."

He searched his stomach. Confirmed. May have skipped breakfast, too.

As a force of habit, he pulled out his phone and checked the GoFundMe for Em. They still had miles to go but had collected a few thousand dollars. He spotted a new comment from someone who had donated $10 to the cause.

> ColinAnderson: Hey, aren't you the guy who's doing that play? Any chance I could meet up with you? Maybe at TSC? I have a story that funnily relates to money, given the whole GoFundMe thing.

NOAH'S STOMACH SOURED, YET ANOTHER PERSON HE'D HAVE to turn down. After he'd tried to find any theater in Indiana and his hometown that'd rent out their space for him to put on his play—even investigating odd venues such as outdoor amphitheaters and hillsides in national parks...

He'd learned that either:

A. The theater wanted to approve the play. I.e., it had to be published. OR
B. The spaces that would let him perform would charge him hundreds of dollars to rent out the place for practices, money he didn't have, nor would have in any near future.

. . .

After discovering this, he'd lied to the people who approached him with their stories. Said they were full on stories, but he'd be happy to lend a sympathetic ear if they needed to get something off their chests.

In his periphery, Harmony narrowed her eyes. She must've caught a glimpse of his phone screen.

"So." She drew out the word. "You have been hanging out with Em a lot, I presume?" She flicked the carrot nose on her onesie in what could only be described as a scorned manner.

"Actually, no. We've not crossed paths a lot this year."

This earned an approving nod from Harmony. She cleared her throat. "Well, let's not talk about Em—"

...you brought her up.

"Oh, how's that play going?! I thought of another idea from one of my exes. If you have the space for it, that is."

Goodness, how many exes did she have? Harmony had already shared ten stories with him.

"Oh, uh." He glanced at his hands and sighed. "I'm going to be honest, Harmony, all my performance venues have fallen through. I don't know if there's going to *be* a play."

Harmony's eyebrows—which she had painted green for some reason—drew together. She rubbed her chin and tsked her tongue.

"That's too bad. I know a lot of people were excited about that. I've heard a lot of people ask about when it's happening since there's not a whole lot of time left in the school year."

"Yeah? Have they been asking you?"

"Nah, I was hiding in some bushes." She shrugged as if this was a normal Tuesday activity for her. He shuddered at the very idea of what Harmony's schedule looked like. It had to be way weirder than that girl who scheduled every fifteen minutes of her life. That had made it into the play.

Guilt corkscrewed in his gut. Now he'd let down all these people.

I should've turned down Sarah in the first place if this thing was destined to fail. Noah buried his face in his hands as the cold, mushy remains of a fry squished in his teeth.

"Do you need a nap?"

He bolted up as Harmony rummaged through a bin full of stuffies, maybe to find him one to cuddle with.

"Erm, no, just upset, I think. Here I have all these stories from guys—and girls—who feel unheard, and they're going to continue to be unheard because I can't get anyone to put on this thing."

Her lips sagged. He realized now that she'd also painted those in green.

"That does sound awful. But maybe you already did them a favor. I mean." She touched her chest, where one of the "coal" buttons rested. "When I'd told you about some of my exes, it was so nice to get it out in the open."

"Yeah, but..." He shook his head. "That's not enough. I'm expected to tell their stories. To be their spokesperson."

She nodded, scanning the ceiling, maybe for the right words, or maybe because Harmony liked to look in random directions to "throw people off her scent and always keep them guessing."

"True. And if you can't perform it sometime this year, I know it'll be disappointing. But I bet you'll eventually put it on."

He sat straighter. Tilted his head.

"What do you mean?" He swirled another fry in the dip and crunched on it. Bad idea; it had already gone cold. "I haven't even landed a job at a theater. I can't barge into one and ask them to do my play if they don't know me."

"Yeah, and maybe you won't put on your play this year or this decade...but if you want it badly enough, you'll eventually be able to air out these stories. I mean." She snickered. "I don't think these dating problems are going away anytime soon."

Harmony leaned over and pulled out a tattered copy of *Emma.*

"I've been reading through this for a class, and either Austen was making fun of the dating conventions of her time...or she hated picnics."

"Picnics?"

"Yeah, there's a whole picnic scene where DRAMA goes down." She flashed jazz hands. "But I have a strong feeling it may be the first one. The dating thing. And the funny thing is." She tapped her nose. "Not much has changed. I have a feeling that play is going to be relevant for a long time."

He scanned the dusty carpet as he mulled this over in his thoughts.

Maybe he hadn't failed. At least, not yet.

Stories got told eventually, and when he had the funds or the position at a theater to do so, he'd tell the stories of these men.

"So what you're saying is, I am ultimately doing good for these people? Even if it takes some time to do so?"

Harmony the Snowman shrugged. "Some of the best things are worth waiting for."

As he bounced off the couch, he grabbed his phone to type out a reply to Colin in the comments. At the door, he turned around and dipped a grateful nod at Harmony.

"Thanks. I think you just lifted something that's been weighing on me for months."

"And that." She pointed at him. "Is exactly what you're doing for those people. Now go get them, tiger! And...avoid picnics." She shook her head, eyes wide. "Dangerous business."

16
IN A RICH MAN'S WORLD
COLIN

"Watcha working on?" I ask.

Noah snaps the laptop shut in TSC and flips around in his high-top chair. He lets out a sigh of relief.

"Sorry, I thought you were someone else." He reopens his HP and shows me a GoFundMe page. "I don't know if you know Emerson."

"The matchmaker girl?" I shove my hands in my hoodie pockets and watch a horde of females pass by, all carrying TSC's poor excuse for sushi. This school doesn't exactly get rave reviews for its attempts at ethnic foods from outside the borders of Indiana.

Great. My nostrils flare. *I'm starting to sound like her.*

"Yeah, the matchmaker one. I'm hoping to get her out of a really bad bet." Noah tilts forward in his chair, hunched over the laptop. He types away at a description for the GoFundMe page. I've learned the ins and outs of that site like my life depended on it. Teachers always have to ask people to fund supplies for their classrooms.

I learned the hard way freshman year, when we shadowed

teachers at the local schools, that most educators provide their own materials for their classes. There's a lot of money that goes into jobs that don't pay well.

"Bad bet?" I remember the GoFundMe. I contributed ten dollars to it, but Noah might not remember me. He looks worn down.

Noah rolls his eyes. "Long story, but she's my best friend, and I want to help her pay off her student loans."

I eye the target amount for the GoFundMe page, tens of thousands of dollars. I doubt even the richest students here living off Daddy's money could cough up that kind of cash.

Or even if they could, I think of Addie; they'd probably be too absorbed in something else to care.

But I guess you have to start somewhere.

A black wallet digs out of my pocket. "I might be able to contribute some." Some more than ten dollars, that is. I've given this some thought, and ever since Noah responded to my comment on the GoFundMe, I'm ready to do this.

Noah passes me an appreciative nod. "Thanks, man."

"How does a thousand dollars sound?"

His eyes swell. "Umm, are you sure? Aren't you a...?"

He stops himself, but I can finish the sentence in my head. An education major. Next to English majors, we're the most notorious for the worst ROI on our college degrees. Especially since I'm planning to teach the Bible to middle schoolers, I can, at best, expect a $50k salary in a richer city that can afford it.

I shrug. Something about this feels good. Feels like a dig back at...

Well, I don't want to think about her.

"I recently came into ten thousand dollars. Well, I got ten thousand dollars back that I had spent," I clarify.

"Oh?" His eyelids pinch nearly shut. I've got his attention. The number one forte of a future teacher: to hold the interest of a crowd. "Hey, didn't you contribute $10 and wanted to hit me up with your story? Sorry I haven't gotten back to you on that yet. Busy, busy, you know?"

"No worries, man." Good to know he would get back to me eventually. "So about that ten thousand, most of that needs to go to loans. But I can spare ten percent for the GoFundMe page. Think of it as an investment in her business since I should've gone to her in the first place."

At the time I met Addie, I'd figured Em charged way too steep a price to pair me with the right person at Mansfield. Now, I wish I could get that investment, all those hours, back and redo it all.

Noah blows out a long breath. "I don't know, man. I'm doing this GoFundMe page to sorta get her away from that matchmaking thing. I don't think an investment in her business is what I'm going for here."

"Either way, I know what it's like to be down on your luck when it comes to funds." I wave the wallet. "A thousand dollars, take it or leave it."

Noah cringes. "She hurt you that badly, huh?"

"What?"

"Dude, people usually don't make impulsive decisions like this without going through a breakup. Do you know how many guys I see pumping iron like crazy at the gym the minute their girlfriends break it off? Besides." He passes me a significant glance. "The two of you went everywhere together."

My guts twist. Should I tell him about Addie? I know I'd commented on the GoFundMe and all, but my veins now are freezing with shock, with hesitancy. She'd probably post a whole video about it while reviewing some local ramen joint. "What I Eat in a Day Putting My Ex on Blast."

Did I care if she did?

"Do you still want me to tell you the story?"

He shrugs. "If you want. We don't even have to include it in the play if you're worried about someone getting mad. Maybe you can decide after if it's worth donating to the fund. Don't get me wrong." He holds his hands up. "I'm all for helping Em. But just chucking money at things isn't going to help you get over this."

I sigh.

No, it's not.

"How long you got?" Before he answers, I slide into the seat opposite him. "I think it could add a fun little spice to your play." Whether I donate or not, I'd at least like to help Noah out for letting me get this off my chest.

He smiles and leans back. "This is going to be good."

* * *

"YOUR CAR OR MINE?" ADDIE STOOD OUTSIDE OF MY DORM and batted those blonde eyelashes at me. She drove me crazy when she did stuff like that.

"Erm." My keys had already jiggled in my pocket, but she'd complained the last few times we'd driven in my car. The thing didn't have heat. Or AC. So, in all seasons, it made for miserable drives. "Yours is fine."

She beamed at me and led me to the parking lot behind her dorm. I whistled when I spotted her vehicle. For some reason, every time I saw it, it surprised me. Maybe because most kids on campus drove run-down vehicles, and the silver, sleek physique on this car screamed of Daddy's money.

"Even with your dad's investment business, I don't know how he afforded something like this to give you." I slipped into the front seat of the electric car. I always wondered where on earth she would charge this in Indiana; maybe in the big city. She did make trips to Muncie a lot when I got overwhelmed with grading papers for student teaching.

She shrugged and giggled, wrapping a coil of blonde hair around her finger as she slid into the driver's seat. "It's nice, right?"

It felt so weird to go from a coughing and sputtering engine to such a quiet drive. I frowned when we passed by the local ice cream joint.

"Aren't we going to go there?"

She jerked her head and flipped on the turn blinker as we glided onto the highway. "I'm tired of going to the same restaurants. Muncie has much better stuff, and I need new content for the page. I can only get my fans so excited about Mansfield ice cream so many times."

Ah, yes, for her foodie page on social media.

I followed her when we started dating, and she'd accumulated a good 5,000 followers since she created the page last year. Not bad, in my opinion, in such a saturated market. But every waking moment was spent growing her following.

I couldn't even remember half the time what she majored in. I doubted she cared.

She wasn't paying for the degree, after all.

Muncie was a forty-five-minute drive. She hunkered down at a charging station in the city (I guess they had one), and then we slid into a parking lot for a fancy Japanese restaurant. Everyone who stepped inside the doors wore suits and bandage dresses. I glanced at my flannel and jeans.

Severely underdressed.

Addie didn't seem to care. She'd be in front of the camera, anyway. After she had parked, she handed me her phone, and I filmed her walking into the restaurant as she did a little twirl right before entering.

We stepped inside, and I grimaced at the dim lighting. Places like this wouldn't even put dollar signs on the menu.

My wallet suddenly felt two pounds lighter in my pocket. "Addie, are you sure we can afford this?"

She cut me a severe look, and it softened moments later. Right, I was supposed to be filming everything. I straightened her phone, and she turned her back to the camera, still talking to me. She'd edit the audio later.

"Don't worry. Dad can handle this bill."

Her father always seemed to take care of the check on our dates.

One time, I'd begged her, for the sake of my manhood, to let me pay for a night out at the movies. She acquiesced but then seemed to get upset that we couldn't get the gourmet popcorn that came in cheddar cheese flavor, nor could we get a sampling of every food item at the concessions stand for her to do a "Trying All the Snacks at a Local Theater" video.

We let her dad pay for all the rest of the dates after that.

Once we took our seats, she ordered for the two of us. Addie knew I'd pale if I looked at menu prices, and since I wasn't picky when it came to food, she let her more "sophisticated palate" decide our entrees for the evening.

The server returned with sashimi minutes later, along with some Shirley Temples.

I sipped on the grenadine soda and took a bite of buttery, raw salmon. *Man, this blows our school's sushi out of the water.* On occasion, I understood her obsession with trying good foods. And I had to admit, it made for fun dates.

Addie refused to eat until I filmed her taking a bite. She made sure I never got her swallowing on camera. Said she looked "gross" when she did that. If I accidentally filmed too long, she'd edit out her gulping down food.

After getting enough B-reel, we could chow down on the rest of our food.

"So." She placed her hands under her chin. "Haven't heard from you much this week. How's life been?"

I smiled, finally, some normal conversation that didn't

have to do with analytics or SEO. "Good. Sorry, student teaching's been running me into the ground."

She squeezed my hand. "Isn't it crazy? Our future is so close. To think we're about to be adults, working adult jobs and doing adult things."

Well, we had been adults already for four years. We'd be set to graduate within a few months. But college did have a way of stalling the bitter realities that came with a 9 to 5.

"Yeah." I grinned. "Speaking of the future, I've been trying to figure out where to apply for teaching positions. They're going to start posting more jobs come May."

Since we lived within thirty minutes of each other's hometowns, that made it easier.

"Where have you been applying, Addie? For..." Again, I blanked on her major. Business-something, I think? She seldom talked about it. "For jobs, anyway? Maybe I can try to get one close to where you are."

I already had a ten-thousand-dollar ring set to arrive in the campus mail within a week. We'd talked about the proposal since the fall semester, and she'd more than hinted at the kind of ring she wanted. I couldn't afford some of her top choices, but I did manage to save enough for a brilliant piece of jewelry. I also scheduled a dozen reservations at restaurants in the Muncie area that she'd enjoy for that evening. Knowing her, she'd want me to film the whole thing.

"Oh." Her hands fanned and fluttered until they settled on the table. She took a bite of uni, sea urchin, sashimi. "I was hoping to try to expand the travel blog thing once I graduated." She puckered her lips in a pout, perhaps anticipating my disappointment. "I'm so close to breaking 6k, and when I reach 10, it's going to be unstoppable from there."

The tuna in my mouth turned to sand.

I'd always thought she'd keep doing this food thing on the

side, but as a full-time thing? With no backup plans? Had she even done any internships?

I spent so many summers mowing lawns and working retail jobs that I didn't have a chance to ask her if she was clocking in anywhere.

"Erm, I think it's great that you want to be an influencer and all, but...shouldn't we have a backup plan in case?" Teaching wouldn't pay enough for the two of us, after all.

And she'd never mentioned wanting kids. I could go either way on that. Considering I'd corralled middle schoolers for years, maybe I didn't want to dive right into that world, either.

But even with just two people, a teacher's salary wouldn't cut it in most places.

Before she could respond, a server returned with the check.

"I'm sorry," the woman in red lipstick told us. "The card has been declined."

Cold panic seized me. Addie paled; then, pink returned to her cheeks. "That can't be right." She held up a phone that she dug out of some kind of designer purse. "Mind if I call someone?"

"Go right ahead." The server placed the unpaid check on the table. Everything writhed within me to look at it, to take in the damage. But I didn't think I wanted to know.

Addie left for a long time. I stared at the rest of the uneaten food and wondered if we could knock something off the bill to make up for what we didn't consume. I'd just dropped ten grand on a ring, after all. I doubted I could afford McDonald's at this point.

Addie returned, and I couldn't tell if she had a smile or grimace on her face.

"Okay, so the good news is it's a mistake. He's wiring some money to me now." Her phone dinged. "There. That should more than cover it. I do know the restaurant takes Apple Pay."

I drew in a sharp breath. "The bad news?"

"So apparently, he pulled the trigger too early." She tossed up air quotes. "He's supposed to take away all bank privileges when you propose since I'm going to be joining a new family unit, and so that means I manage my finances, and apparently, you're proposing sometime soon. He got the dates mixed up and canceled my card connected to his bank today by accident."

My eyebrows furrowed. Bank privileges?

"Did you know he'd do this?"

She let out a frustrated sigh. "No, not really. I mean, Mom and Dad said something about weaning me off. Just because I'm their only child doesn't mean they'd pay for things forever. But I figured it would be a several-year process. Kids can stay on their parents' insurance until they're, like, twenty-six, so I think I figured they'd give me that long."

Had she never thought to check with them?

Then again, Addie had never been one to ever think far ahead. If a need ever arose, someone else would take care of it for her.

Did that mean she expected me to...?

"Addie, does this mean you're going to apply to some jobs? Because although a teacher's salary could help us get by for a few months, it's going to be..."

She pursed her lips and held up a finger. "I wondered if Mom and Dad were going to do something like this. Well, not *this* exactly, but I can tell they've been getting jittery about a few of my shopping sprees." She'd dropped $900 at Victoria's Secret last weekend, or so her receipt told me when she showed me her recent mall trip. "So I'm already ahead of you on brainstorming a solution."

I straightened in my seat until the plush fabric of the booth met my back. *Well, that's a surprise.*

"So you know how Dad has that investing firm? Where his workers work on commission, and they usually start making six figures within the first couple of years? He's constantly looking for people to fill positions as sales representatives. Usually, within the first six months, people start making a salary. Some top performers even get millions within the first five years on commission."

I felt myself brighten.

Of course!

Maybe Addie didn't apply for jobs because she knew she'd have one at her dad's company. Sure, commission-based pay was less than ideal, but when she set her mind to something, she could make it happen. I bet she'd be a top performer within the first six months.

We could do six months on just one salary. We could make that work.

And if Addie made enough money after a year or two, she could save up to do a year's worth of traveling for her foodie blog. She'd always have a job to come back to at her dad's company if things didn't work out.

"Addie, you'd do amazing at that." I squeezed her hands, but they slackened in my grip. Maybe she was scared about her first job. "I'll support you one hundred percent. Sometimes, you have to start with something else before you can get to what you want."

She jerked her head, and she cringed. "I was thinking that *you* could take that job."

Everything in me went cold.

Sure, yes, for her, I'd do anything. But why did I go five figures into debt for a teaching degree if I wouldn't go into that field? I'd felt a clear calling from God to teach the Bible since my sophomore year of high school.

"But." I frowned. "That doesn't make a lot of sense, love. That would mean neither of us would be getting paid for six months."

Her face scrunched more. "I mean, we do have the foodie page, and I have an account my parents invested in for me since birth. We could dip into that for a few months while you get up and running at Dad's company. And we're so close to getting it to 10k. Once we pass that, I can start getting sponsorships and..."

She kept talking, but I didn't hear the words.

A buzz filled my brain as the hours spent teaching, the students who said they wanted to become teachers because of me, the unnecessary course load crammed into eight semesters so I could graduate on time...

"Addie." My voice turned stern. "I want to support your dreams, I do. But don't you think that marriage is going to require sacrifice on both of our parts? What if you took that job, and if you hate it after a year, we could figure out something else? Maybe you'd make enough in that first year to be able to take a year off after that and travel and food blog."

Something in her broke.

I saw it. Something in her eyes shattered, and I knew I wasn't going to repair the pieces.

She released her grip, drew herself up, and turned cold.

"I'm sorry, but my dream is to travel and food blog. I don't want to put it off for a year and let the page suffer because I'm not posting enough. If you can't support that, emotionally or financially, maybe I don't know you as well as I thought."

It took several seconds for me to comprehend fully what she'd meant.

She was willing to give me up...for a food blog.

Fine.

"Yeah." I stood from the table and pulled up the contacts

for a friend in Muncie. I could crash at his place tonight and arrange a ride for the next day. "Maybe we don't know each other well at all."

Within a week, we broke up.

And within another two weeks, I got the money back for the ring.

Within one day after we split, she'd posted a foodie video: "What I Eat in a Day after I've Been Broken Up With."

She got to 6k with that video.

Then, her account got hacked a month later, and she lost all her followers.

17
VALENTINE'S DAY
NOAH

Leave it to Professor Reed to have rehearsal on Valentine's Day AND the day of the lip sync battle.

Noah stole a sneaky glance at his phone as Professor Reed reviewed notes for the latest scenes they'd done. They planned on taking a break after this and would resume practice about an hour after.

He hoped it would give him enough time to swing by TSC and watch Em and her group perform.

Heat crawled up his cheeks at the thought of her. The other day, Harmony had run into him in the communications building and had waggled her brows when she heard he would do his best to attend.

"Ooo, you do know that our dance is all about proposing, right?"

He'd shuffled uncomfortably away. "Erm, Harmony, you do realize we are just friends, yes?"

After Harmony had given up her flirting phase with him, he could finally relax around her. But every so often, he worried.

"Relax." She punched his shoulder, but not in her usual

flirty way. This punch lacked pizazz. "I have my eyes on a certain beauty in a trench coat." She giggled. "And besides, everyone knows about your crush on Em."

He shrunk into his sweater.

"Everyone?"

Harmony procured a magnifying glass from the pockets of her harem pants. She stared at him, enlarging her eyes.

"I had a Sherlock phase, good sir; I did my homework." She stashed the glass away. "But even if I hadn't, yeah, it's obvious. Except maybe to her."

At least he could relax at that. Em, although observant when it came to pairing couples, wasn't always the best at self-awareness. She'd told him so many embarrassing stories of when she tried to put herself out there at the beginning of the year during Welcome Weekend events.

"Let's just say that your girl can't flirt to save your life," Em'd confided to him shortly after that event.

Now, back in the present, Professor Reed told him to emphasize a different word in one of his lines as part of her rehearsal notes.

"Okay." She set her clipboard down on the stage and clapped her hands. "That concludes the first half of rehearsal. And—"

A flurry of movement and a cacophony of noise flooded the space. Backpack zippers sang in a hurry, and Weston darted for the double doors that led out into the hallway—much like a scuba diver who'd run out of oxygen and needed to surface.

Noah rose to follow, but Professor Reed jabbed a finger at him.

"You."

He sighed. "Me?"

Of course his plans to watch Em in her dance competition would get waylaid.

"Yes." She stooped and picked up a stack of fliers. "Any chance you could hang these during the break?"

Excuses flurried his mind as he fought back the images of his first week this school year, hanging similar posters in TSC. Professor Reed turned her eyes doe-y—a scary mental image, and he acquiesced.

"Sure, but I do need to take care of something first."

He grabbed the stack of papers from her, headed to the hallway, and dumped them on a side table. Doubting that anyone would purloin such worthless treasures, he headed down the hall toward the doors that would lead to TSC.

A familiar figure surfaced, and he stopped in his tracks.

"Sarah?" He tilted his head. "Are you ever at *your* theater?"

She snickered. "Yeah, I guess I am here a lot, aren't I?"

"Here for costumes?"

"Actually." She lifted a finger and then aimed it at him. "I'm here for you."

This staggered him, and he could've sworn he backed away a couple of inches. Why couldn't she call? Or text?

She laughed again. "Kidding, I am here to watch a friend of mine in the lip sync battle but had been told by someone in line that you were at rehearsal. Figured I'd knock out both tasks at the same time."

She must've asked the person in the queue seconds before they were let into TSC auditorium because the dance had already started. Thankfully, Em's group didn't go in the lineup first. He'd have enough time to sneak in, watch her performance, and duck out.

"Okay." He shoved his hands into his pockets. "What are you here to see me for?"

Sarah bounced up and down, shaking her fists in excitement. "So I'm sorry for not contacting you about this sooner, but I had to be certain. That play. Yours. We want it. And if you're still up for it, we'd like to perform it for that grant."

His heart missed several beats and now thrummed erratically in his neck. He sucked in a deep breath and let it out.

"But...what about Simon?"

Sarah rolled her eyes. "I met with the board separately, and we all agreed. Simon has been acting like he's the president. Simon recently directed a play, and the cast was so unhappy with how controlling he was that we had several telling us they would no longer audition for us. It was the last straw."

Huh, so the technical director of the theater occasionally directed shows. *Good to know.* He penciled in that fact for later.

"So he's not working there anymore?" *AKA, Sarah, can you get me a job, pleaseandthankyou?*

Sarah pulled a sour face. "Not exactly. He's camping out in the position for now, but I believe our president is planning to approach him when we reach a lull in the season. A month or so from now."

Maybe I could ask to apply then. He still hadn't managed to secure a position for when he graduated. Pressure built daily to where he couldn't sleep at night unless he popped a melatonin gummy. The lack of sleep worked with the erratic rehearsal schedule that sometimes went on until 2 a.m.

"Gotcha." He bobbled on his heels. "So, you're interested in the play?"

Her face lit up again. "Yes! I will say." She wagged a finger. "We do still need a happy story in it. One that doesn't end in a breakup."

Got it. He'd have to locate a success story and write about that.

I mean, if you make a move on Em soon, maybe YOU can be the success story.

Whoa, whoa, whoa, *pump the brakes.*

His mind argued back. *Dude, you've been pumping the brakes so much that your car has stalled. It's okay to start with something. Even five mph.*

Memories surged of his first time driving. His mom gripped the handlebar of the car until her knuckles bleached white. He hadn't gone over ten miles per hour in the parking lot, but she'd said it felt like 85.

Baby steps.

He realized he'd gone seconds without replying to Sarah. "I think I can make that work."

"Great!" She eeped. "I look forward to seeing that final draft from you soon since we will need to start getting the other pieces in place. The performance is a few months from now, but as you know, that time disappears like that." She snapped her fingers and then threw a wave at him. "Probably should get back to the lip sync battle."

"I'm headed that way." He followed her.

They talked details on the way over, and lightheartedness filled his chest. At long last, the stories of those men would be heard. Seen. Experienced. And more importantly, talked about.

Harmony was right. The right opportunity would arise. He'd expected it a decade from now, but he wouldn't complain. He gazed heavenward and tossed up a silent thank you.

No seats were available by the time they got into the auditorium, so they sat in the sloping aisles, where other students clustered. Mean of the school to still charge them the same admission as the students who got real seats.

They held chapels in this same space, and the school claimed they didn't make the chapels necessary because they "know the students care about their spiritual growth." In reality, they didn't have enough seats for the population at the school.

Not that he minded.

From his vantage point, he managed to watch Em leap into the arms of a dance partner during Katy Perry's "Firework." He whooped, but his voice was lost in the sea of hollers from the audience.

Although not the best performance he'd witnessed over the years of lip sync battles—usually, a group that picked a popular movie at the time for their theme won—he had to give them credit. For a gaggle of students with no dance experience, they could give the principal dancers from the theater a run for their money.

That is if any of us had money.

Student debt would soon drown them.

Speaking of, he'd planned to show Em the GoFundMe page soon. With the help of the marketing department, he'd managed to get $9000 in donations. Not enough to cover her bet, but it was a start.

He slipped out after the performance to go tack posters at the theater. Professor Reed had rushed toward him and pointed in the direction of the props loft.

"Any chance you could run up there and do some inventory?" She handed him a clipboard. "You don't have to grab anything yet, just to make sure we have enough to incorporate props in our next rehearsal."

Ever the people-pleaser, he agreed and headed upstairs to choke on the dust that added a thin layer of dirt to everything. After fifteen or twenty minutes, he returned downstairs, only to find Em and the stage manager in the hallway.

The stage manager eyed him and her and then dipped out of the conversation, passing him a knowing wink.

Maybe Harmony is right, maybe everyone knows.

Conversation died on their lips, and Em wouldn't look him in the eye. He checked his phone. Had just enough time to slip back into his dorm and grab a snack before the break ended.

Em held up a hand. “Noah, I have something to say.”

And then she said it. Releasing her foot off the brakes. She liked him back.

I...I think I finally have that happy story for Sarah. At least, he hoped.

18

THE LIE

NOAH

"Thanks for being here, Em."

Noah squeezed Em's hand in the lobby of the community theater. Everything stunk of musk and dust and stale popcorn from past shows. It had been a few months since they had hosted a performance here, and he could tell they hadn't vacuumed the splotchy red carpeting in a while.

Em squeezed his hand back and sank onto a bench near the theater's double doors.

Muffled conversation sounded from within. Sarah had mentioned something about the first five minutes being dedicated to logistics. Then they'd...he let out a rattled breath... invite him in.

"Honestly, it'll give me some breathing room." Em dug into her bag and flipped open a laptop. "With my interview at campus tomorrow, it may be best to step away from school grounds. Being there's gotten me all jittery."

Thanks to Harmony's digging into the school's unfortunate PR issues and airing them out in the school newspaper, Em scored an interview for a PR/marketing position at Mansfield. And even though Noah knew Em could do the whole thing blindfolded and with sleep deprivation and still nail it, that wouldn't help ease her nerves now.

So he'd invited her to attend the board meeting where they'd discuss his play. If anything, to get her away from the campus bubble. But it wouldn't hurt to have someone to cheer him on for the production of his first written play.

He sat beside Em and took out his computer as well.

Em quirked a brow. "Last-minute exam study?"

He shook his head. Theater majors' finals included performances and audition pieces, which had already taken place. Theater professors tended to show movies for the last few classes since the school still required them to attend those.

"Still need to work on that last scene." He grinned at her. "The happily ever after one."

"Oh?" She simpered. "Got a lead for that one?"

He scooted closer and banded an arm around her, squeezing. "Maybe."

It took her a second to register. Then her eyes widened.

"Oh."

He couldn't tell if she sounded surprised. Scared. Happy? Em wasn't always the easiest to read, even after they'd gone on a few dates and, well, been besties for four years.

"Is that a bad thing?"

Em considered this for a moment while biting her bottom lip. Her fingers rubbed on the holes in her jeans. "No, I don't think so. But we're not even married yet. How do you know it's a happily ever after?"

True, but he did have plans to propose soon. Jana's bet or not, he couldn't wait any longer to spend his life with her, especially if he'd stick around for his play to be performed and to help with summer drama camp. Maybe he could get a barista job locally while Em worked at Mansfield.

They'd find a way to make it work. They always did.

"True, we're not. But I have a good feeling."

Her eyes clouded, and she pulled her gaze away. "Yeah."

"Hey."

When she glanced back at him, he pressed his forehead against hers.

"Wanna tell me what's on your mind?"

"My parents." She sighed. "I'm sure there was a period of time where they thought their story was a happy one too."

The divorce was still scarring over.

He watched the wounds slowly heal in the last few months, but he imagined they'd never fully go away. If they committed to each other for life, he'd have to assure her that they wouldn't go down the same path. That he wouldn't transform into her father, and she wouldn't turn into her mother. Or vice versa.

And he was ready for that.

Was she?

"We don't have to do our story, Em."

She shook her head. "You *do* need a happy one that ends with the couple getting and sticking together. You promised Sarah that."

"I know..."

The doors flew open, and Sarah tromped out into the lobby in clunky heels. She nearly tripped and steadied herself on the brick wall next to the doors. Photos from past drama camp performances featuring casts in neon green show T-shirts displayed near Sarah's hands.

Noah bounced up from the bench. "They ready for me?"

Sarah grimaced. "Erm, one of them is taking longer with the logistics portion than I thought they would." Her shoulders scrunched. Why did she look so uncomfortable? The muffled voices had turned to what Noah thought sounded like shouting. "But I thought I could give you some pointers for your presentation. Since you're going to be talking with all the departments about the needs for the show..."

Got it.

His theater classes had prepared him for this. Sometimes, scenic artists and costume designers had a very different vision than that of the director or, in this case, the playwright. He'd have to find compromises and ways to work with the different crew members.

Sarah led him to the green room and shoved a K-cup of tea into a Keurig.

"Need anything to sip on while we wait and go over some last-minute things?"

He glanced at the clock, which read 6:05 p.m. Caffeine at this hour, on top of the jitters?

"No thanks." He sank into a squeaky chair and forced his attention on a whiteboard with lists of supplies the theater needed to acquire for its mainstage summer performance.

"Hey." Her voice mellowed. "You're going to do great. They love you, having worked with you before, and it's a brilliant play."

"Speaking of." A mild panic bit him when he realized he hadn't brought his laptop. He took a deep breath and reminded himself he'd left it in the lobby. "I will have that happy scene, I promise."

She snickered. "I know. You've been blowing up my phone about it. I trust you. Besides, I'm pretty sure Lin Manuel changed things up to the literal last minute for the first performance of *Hamilton*. We can adjust."

Good to know.

"It's just." He sighed, recalling how Em had curled up into herself in the lobby when he had mentioned their happily ever after. "It's mine. The story, I mean"

Sparks lit up in Sarah's eyes.

"Ooh, spill." Hot tea steamed into a mug. She scooped up the cup handle and sat across from him.

And he did. In brief, he told the story of how they'd gotten together. It had surprised him that he hadn't kept Sarah up-to-date on everything. He'd told the tale so many times that he'd lost count of those who didn't know yet.

"Ooh." Sarah squealed. "That's going to make a beautiful ending scene!" She pumped a fist.

"Right, except..."

He sighed. This sounded terrible right after the very good news he'd shared.

"Em is worried. She's seen a lot of happily ever afters go south. Her parents, some of the people she's matched. What if the play is setting up unrealistic expectations?"

If things didn't work out between him and Em, did he forever immortalize a lie?

"Hmm." Sarah tapped a green-chipped nail on her chin. "You bring up a good point, but I don't think that means you should scrap the scene."

His spine straightened against the chair. He could feel that the padding in it had disintegrated over the years.

"You don't?"

"No, Noah, listen." She sipped from the rim of her mug and grimaced. Too hot, he guessed. "Even the happiest of couples go through rough patches. Romance stories are always a lie because they end the story before it's done."

Fair. He'd watched his brother in a failed relationship that had seemed like the end game. And all the stories he'd heard for this play?

Sarah stood and pinched a honey packet out of a bowl. She tore into a corner and drizzled the amber liquid into her cup as she returned to her seat.

"We love the lie because we love the honeymoon stage. It's when we pretend the world, that life, doesn't exist for a moment. It's why we love to watch plays. Those are a honeymoon stage for us...if even for a few hours."

Noah nodded. Although he'd watched his fair share of tragic shows, they always formed an escape from his realities for a few hours. It was as if he could step out of life, even for one evening.

"But if you tell a lie well." She lifted a finger. "You can sneak some truth in there."

"Truth?"

"Yeah, and in this case, the lie you're telling people in your play is that the story ends when the relationship breaks off or when the couple finally gets together." She leaned forward. "Do you want to know what truth you're telling?"

He felt his chin bob.

How did she know this, and he didn't? He'd written the dang thing.

"You're telling the audience that love takes work. Love is a choice. Love, when done wrong, can destroy a person. But done right." A dreamy look overtook her face. "Is something worth fighting for, and that's why we keep trying. Even when the dating pool gets worse and worse. And people get pettier and more selfish. Because the right people fight for the right things, and when you find that right person..."

Her hands flew into sparks.

"Boom. It gives us hope. And that's the truth you're giving them. Hope."

Weight, from what, he didn't know, lifted off his shoulders. Who knew he could feel this light?

So he had created something worth writing about...to give people a reality check, but more importantly, hope.

A flushed man with a mop of sweaty brown hair appeared in the doorway, panting.

"Oh." Sarah smoothed a wrinkle in her skirt. "Y'all ready for us?"

The man shook his head and held onto his knees while he caught his breath. “Simon, erm, just quit.”

Sarah paled. “Quit?”

Noah’s eyes widened. Sarah hadn’t informed him much of the Simon drama as of late. All he knew was that the board hadn’t yet confronted him on his micromanaging in his last production. They kept putting it off.

“He didn’t like that we were addressing the cast and crew’s concerns, so he stormed out. Said he had plenty of other places clamoring for him and his connections.” The man threw up air quotes. He’d regained his breath. “He was very clear on that last point.”

Sarah took in the information for one second.

And one second only.

Then, she bopped out of her chair and turned to Noah, smiling.

“Well, Noah, I thought this meeting was just going over the logistics of your play.” Her grin turned sly. “But maybe we can talk to the board about that position that opened up.”

19

DATE EXPECTATIONS

NOAH

Backstage, Noah let out a shaky breath. He poked his head through the curtains, a no-no on opening nights. As a thespian, he should've known that. Just seeing the size of the audience could cause any professional to choke and forget their first lines.

But he couldn't help himself.

For an unknown and unpublished play, in the middle of cornfield Indiana, during the off-season (summer break), they'd developed quite an audience. Granted, the performance would happen right after Drama Camp and right before the school year, so plenty of students had hiked up to Mansfield a week early to get set up in the dorms. Plenty of families were still abuzz about the last performance and wanted to support the next one.

Still, to his surprise, the theater burst with a nearly full audience. Townspeople tended to support the few local events they had. Not to mention, plenty of the kiddos he worked with at drama camp gave him rave reviews and said they wanted to watch "Director Noah's" play.

He'd assured the parents that he kept the content PG.

A hand clasped his shoulder, and he jumped. Whirling around, he spotted Em, who had shrunken into her tank top, likely embarrassed for scaring him so much.

"You okay, Noah?"

"Yeah." He eyed the ring on her left finger and breathed. "Yeah, just nerves is all."

He'd sworn she wouldn't let him ask her to marry him for at least a year, what with all the trauma she'd undergone this past year. But two months into summer, with her starting her job at Mansfield and him being available after every rehearsal, things moved faster than expected.

She'd hinted by July that she wanted to start looking at wedding venues.

He wished he hadn't made fun of so many college students for getting together so fast. *When you know...*

Em beamed at him and squeezed his shoulder. There was something so heavenly about that brief moment of touch.

"You're going to do great. You said the dress rehearsal went well, right?"

"Yeah..."

He poked his head out the curtain again. And he spotted, in the front row, the interviewees. He'd asked Sarah if they could get into the show for free. After all, he'd be telling their stories; the least he could do was spot their admission. Almost all of them could make it except for Dylan, the short king, who'd planned to propose to his new girlfriend that very evening. From what Noah had heard, she was over six feet tall.

Dylan had gotten with her right after his interview with Noah.

Noah's eyes swelled when he spotted a familiar figure in the front row. What was Director Jeremy doing here? Yes, he'd sent him the social media invite, but Noah had only gotten the "Read" notification. He'd figured after the brutal divorce that Jeremy would steer clear from anything to do with relationships.

Noah shimmied back behind the curtain to the backstage area, which was cooler due to the lack of stage lights.

"Stop psyching yourself out, love." Em nodded at the curtain. "They're going to think this is great."

"It's not that." He shook his head. "There are people out there who I didn't even think could make it. Is this that important to them?"

Em stared up into his eyes for a moment, and something wistful overtook her pupils, which were shrouded in the near-darkness of the backstage area.

"Permission to nerd out for a moment with you?"

He smirked. "Granted."

"So when I did research on matchmakers for my business and discovered they charge quite literally tens to hundreds of thousands of dollars...I went on a rabbit trail of other expensive businesses."

He crinkled his eyelids. Where was she going with this?

"One other business almost as expensive as matchmaking is ghostwriting. Basically, people writing other people's books for them. Do you want to know how expensive it is to get someone to tell your story?"

He shrugged. He hadn't gone into a Business or Finance major for a reason.

"Tens to hundreds of thousands of dollars."

His eyes swelled again. He went into the wrong career field.

"Granted." She perched a hand on her hip. "Those writers more than earn that pay, but that's how much people's stories are worth to them. They'd give up their entire life savings for their stories to be told."

She slid a hand on his chest, and a warm feeling overtook him.

"And that's what you're doing tonight. You're telling people their stories are worth hearing. I can think of nothing nobler."

The buzz in his brain eased. No matter if the literal curtain caught on fire during the performance tonight, it would all be worth it. People had ached for years for something like this.

Clapping echoed off the walls as the lights underneath the curtain dimmed. He scooped up a microphone on a music stand, let out a long breath, and advanced toward the stage. A spotlight met him in the middle.

"Hey, everyone." He squinted into an audience he could no longer see. Half the auditorium responded with a greeting.

He glanced up at the tech booth and caught Sarah's smile and thumbs-up seconds before Sarah returned to her headset. Probably to get the cues for the first scene ready.

"It's an honor to not only have this play performed but to have been so deeply embedded in the process." He could start to see past the stage light and make out hazy silhouettes. "Most playwrights don't get that chance."

He paced, wishing he'd written this speech on a notecard to have on hand in case he blanked. But he'd probably have dropped the dang thing from nerves.

"But what's the biggest honor is that people let me hear their stories. I've purposely avoided the world of dating until, well." He smirked. "A certain someone just wouldn't let my heart go."

An aw sounded from a few audience members.

He clasped his heart with his free hand and chuckled.

"But I was mostly relying on your," he pointed at the audience, "expertise."

He stopped, planting his feet. This was the most important part, and he couldn't botch it. For all the thousands of lines and monologues he'd memorized over the years, why was this the hardest one to remember?

"If you've been out of the dating sphere for a while, something you should know is it's a hot mess."

Chuckles and an "Amen, brother" whooped.

"I mean, a hot mess. If you haven't even dated in the last five years, count yourselves enormously lucky. Because I wouldn't wish the dating world on my worst enemy."

Sound sobered.

He could hear the uncomfortable shift in seats, maybe from a few married couples who had lucked out, like he had, with love dropping into their laps without a struggle.

"There are lots of reasons we can point to for why it's such a dumpster fire. But instead of talking your ears off, I'm going to let the very real stories I heard speak for themselves. I just hope that you listen, relate, and most importantly, make it your mission to do things a little differently."

He eyed the wings of the stage. Em beamed at him, and he saw the sheen of tears in her waterline.

After all the terrible dating experiences she'd been through this last year, she'd get a chance to commiserate. For a few hours, she could drop the burdens she'd had to carry these last two semesters.

"Because at the end of the day, whether we end up with someone or not, that person we're sitting across from at the coffee shop is, well, a person."

He spotted Chuck in the front row and smiled at him.

"They're someone's daughter. Someone's son. Someone's..."

He locked eyes with Jeremy. A woman sat beside him, with Jeremy's arm draped behind her. Even in the darkness, Noah could tell she had the sweetest eyes in the world, the kind filled with kindness. And Jeremy's were dimmed, but they had a spark of hope in them.

"Someone's future husband."

He'd be that soon for Em, too. The thought both terrified and excited him. If only everyone could understand the responsibility they held when they took on any kind of relationship. How many people wouldn't try if they knew the cost? The hurt they could cause if they tampered with it in the wrong way?

"So make sure to treat them well. Whether you end up with them or not, they'll at least have a good story to tell about you."

The curtains swished behind him. Likely now for the cast in the wings to take their places behind it.

"Without further ado, I introduce you to."

He stared into the light until his eyes watered.

"Date Expectations."

TREY'S AUTHOR NOTE

As a man—a Christian man, to be specific—there are a lot of expectations for men when it comes to dating. Great (date) expectations, if you will. In the dating field, Christian men are typically expected to:

- Make the first move
- Be the one to ask first about a date
- Pay for the first date
- Meet the parents first and quickly
- Fix the problems, even if they didn't create it
- Be level-headed in all stressful situations every time
- Have emotions but do not express them as much, otherwise, it's a turn-off.
- Have every intention only be for marriage, even in the small things
- Give up everything (including interests) to make the other happy
- Be the one to accept responsibility, even if they

didn't do anything wrong to deserve blame or accusations.

This doesn't even count some of the things men don't have control over. For example, men can't control whether they come from a bad home or divorced parents. Men can't control their height. Men can't control or change their past, especially relationship trauma. They have no control over these things, and yet, sometimes, they are passed over in dating because of one or many of these.

From the first few dates to long-term relationships, men are sized up in a lot of things to be and act a certain way, especially in emotionally stressful situations. And if they don't handle it properly, then heaven help them when they get criticized for it by their significant other.

Some suggestions in the bullet points aren't even bad. They're good suggestions. And that's where the problem can be found. What were meant to be suggestions, both women and men (especially older married couples) have made into rules, let alone expect you to follow them. And if you don't like those rules or if you are giving more than receiving back, you are told to "man up." Or worse, if you are being hurt in a relationship, people will think that you deserved it or that you did something to provoke it. After all, since dating leads to marriage, some painfully summarize it as "happy wife, happy life," so you're expected to start on that early on.

When my wife approached me to co-write this book, I wasn't sure at first. "Who am I to say anything on this topic?" was a thought I had, only to realize I have a lot to say in writing. I endured an emotionally scarring breakup in 2018 that was full of gaslighting, ridicule, blame-shifting, and harsh, untruthful words. That resulted in nine months of depression and two years of therapy and additional grief recovery. Furthermore, I thought of how many stories my guy friends and roommates have told me about their dating relationships. Horrible breakups, broken engagements, and even gaslighting experiences. And so, I said yes to writing this book for all the guys and myself that went unheard. When I wrote my first chapter (chapter 3), I realized not only could I write, but I could write well and bring these real stories to life.

The point of this novella is not to blame women, nor is it saying, "Listen to all men." The point coincides with the *Matchmaker* tie-in novel: Both sides can be hurt, and both sides can be ruthless. So if you, as a man, have been hurt in a relationship, if you have been strung along, gaslit, defamed, and even stalked, I hope this book speaks the story you weren't or aren't able to share. From one man to another, I understand. I hear you, and I see you.

HOPE'S AUTHOR'S NOTE

When I originally penned *Matchmaker*, I thought of a quote from Jane Austen. When interviewed about why she never wrote from a male POV, she essentially said something along the lines of: "Well, I'm not a male, so I don't know what they say in close circles."

Don't completely quote me on that because I don't want to sully the beautiful words of a literary great. But considering *Matchmaker*, based on *Emma*, was from a female POV—and it included my experiences of going on dates with 50+ men—I still lacked in the male POV. Although I'd heard anecdotes, I didn't know what it was like to be a guy trying to navigate the waters of relationships.

So I approached my husband, then-fiance at the time, to see if he'd be open to co-authoring a book from the POV of the male love interest from *Matchmaker*.

Hence why this novella was born.

Men and women go through a diverse range of experiences in the dating world. What seemed to stand out to both of us were the expectations. Yes, expectations for females (ridiculous ones at that, I might say)...but I'd covered those in length in *Matchmaker*.

We wanted to touch on the "date" expectations placed on guys.

The pressure to provide.

The pressure to sacrifice.

The pressure to make the first move.

The pressure to fix everything that goes wrong.

The list goes on, but we wanted to offer both perspectives to fully round out the idea that dating in the Christian world is super messed up. We would do well to undermine these toxic behaviors and encourage healthy relationships.

We hope that in both stories, many people feel heard and seen. Unfortunately, we can't include everything that can go wrong in a Christian relationship, or that book would be roughly 1,000 pages long, and it would be extremely expensive to print.

But just like with Noah, we hope that some stories felt heard and seen.

Now, let's do it differently.

And let's see people as human beings.

As future husbands, future wives.

And most importantly, as made in the image of God. If we damage God's image, we can imagine God won't take that lightly.

DISCUSSION QUESTIONS

For book clubs or personal reflection. There shouldn't be too many spoilers ahead, but it doesn't hurt to read these after finishing the book.

1. What are "date expectations" placed on different people? How can it look different, depending on your sex?
2. What is the difference between a preference and a non-negotiable? Should we allow preferences to get in the way (height, salary, etc.) of a relationship that could be a good fit for us?
3. Why is it important for our stories to be told? Why do we gravitate toward works of fiction that we can relate to?
4. Why do you believe the world of dating is such a "dumpster fire"? How can we improve how we approach relationships?
5. What are the double standards we see in dating, such as Millie being allowed to experience emotions but Jeremy not being able to? How can

we have a more objective approach when it comes to our standards?

6. What are some toxic behaviors that one sex can get away with that another one can't? Provide examples from all perspectives.
7. When Noah approaches his professor about the play, he gets shut down because it could be viewed as anti-feminine. Why is it that we typically avoid difficult dating stories from men's perspectives?
8. In what ways can the expressions "man up," "shake it off," and "take it like a man" affect men in dating? Where can it get precarious when it comes to stalking and Title IX issues?
9. Why are stories that end at happily ever after considered "lies"? How can we integrate more truth into the ways we talk about our relationships, past and present?
10. Why do you think that most people nowadays have a "horror story" when it comes to dating? How can we adapt our behavior on dates to prevent more of these horror stories from happening, whether or not we end up with said person?
11. Why does money play such a big role in relationships? Why are men typically seen as providers, and where do the expectations for this become unrealistic?
12. Why do you think all sexes tend to be afraid of commitment (or too eager to commit before someone else is ready)?
13. Why do "users" exist in dating relationships (people who use people as "boy toys," for instance)? How can we avoid becoming this in our relationships?

14. What is a healthy "pace" for a relationship? Why does this differ from couple to couple?
15. How has social media impacted how we view relationships? Should couples be more honest on social media about their struggles? Why or why not?

www.ingramcontent.com/pod-product-compliance
Lightning Source LLC
Chambersburg PA
CBHW072237190626
46809CB00018B/2686

* 9 7 8 1 9 6 8 5 7 5 0 2 1 *